19

KI KAWAHARA ABEC BEE-PEE

SWORD ART ONLINE
MOON CRADLE

SWORD ART ONLINE

"N-no, that can't be...!"

Ronie Arabel § Formerly Kirito's page at the academy. In recognition of her deeds during the war, she is now an apprentice Integrity Knight at Central Cathedral.

"At this rate, there's going to be another war."

Kirito § The boy who brought peace to the Underworld. Presently, he serves as the swordsman delegate on Centoria's Human Unification Council.

"It's impossible...So long as the Law of Power exists, no darklander can kill a resident of the human realm."

Iskahn § During the war, he was the head of the pugilists guild in the Dark Army. He is currently attempting to establish a peaceful exchange with the human realm as commander of the Dark Territory.

"If the true culprit is from the human realm, that would mean they are capable of ignoring the Taboo Index."

Sheyta Synthesis Twelve § An Integrity Knight formerly known as Sheyta the Silent. After the war, she married her combat partner, Iskahn. She now resides in Obsidia, where she is the human realm's ambassador plenipotentiary.

Human Unification Council

Swordsman Delegate Kirito

Swordswoman Subdelegate Asuna

Integrity Knight Fanatio

Integrity Knight Deusolbert

Apprentice Integrity Knight Ronie

Apprentice Integrity Knight Tiese

Flatland Goblins' Domain

Northern Cave

Mountain Goblins' Domain

Rulid Village

Orcs' Domain

Eastern Gate

People of Darkness's Domain

Human Realm

Central Cathedral

Obsidia Palace

Dark Territory

Giants' Domain

Ogres' Domain

After the war, work began on forging a dialogue between the human realm and the Dark Territory, as propounded by Kirito and Iskahn, the two sides' delegates. The human realm began accepting tourists from the Dark Territory, and the Dark Territory started receiving merchant caravans from the human realm.

World's End Altar

Dark Territory Headquarters

Commander Iskahn

Ambassador Sheyta

Real World

Alice

Leafa

Sinon

Lisbeth, Silica, Klein, Agil

Illustration: Tatsuya Ki

SWORD ART ONLINE
moon cradle

VOLUME 19

Reki Kawahara

abec

bee-pee

YEN ON

NEW YORK

SWORD ART ONLINE, Volume 19: MOON CRADLE
REKI KAWAHARA

Translation by Stephen Paul
Cover art by abec

This book is a work of fiction. Names, characters, places, and incidents are the product of the author's imagination or are used fictitiously. Any resemblance to actual events, locales, or persons, living or dead, is coincidental.

SWORD ART ONLINE Vol.19
©Reki Kawahara 2017
Edited by Dengeki Bunko
First published in Japan in 2017 by KADOKAWA CORPORATION, Tokyo.
English translation rights arranged with KADOKAWA CORPORATION, Tokyo, through Tuttle-Mori Agency, Inc., Tokyo.

English translation © 2020 by Yen Press, LLC

Yen On
150 30th Street, 19th Floor
New York, NY 10001

Visit us at yenpress.com
facebook.com/yenpress
twitter.com/yenpress
yenpress.tumblr.com
instagram.com/yenpress

First Yen On Edition: April 2020

Yen On is an imprint of Yen Press, LLC.
The Yen On name and logo are trademarks of Yen Press, LLC.

The publisher is not responsible for websites (or their content) that are not owned by the publisher.

Library of Congress Cataloging-in-Publication Data
Names: Kawahara, Reki, author. | Abec, 1985– illustrator. | Paul, Stephen, translator.
Title: Sword art online / Reki Kawahara, abec ; translation, Stephen Paul.
Description: First Yen On edition. | New York, NY : Yen On, 2014–
Identifiers: LCCN 2014001175 | ISBN 9780316371247 (v. 1 : pbk.) |
    ISBN 9780316376815 (v. 2 : pbk.) | ISBN 9780316296427 (v. 3 : pbk.) |
    ISBN 9780316296434 (v. 4 : pbk.) | ISBN 9780316296441 (v. 5 : pbk.) |
    ISBN 9780316296458 (v. 6 : pbk.) | ISBN 9780316390408 (v. 7 : pbk.) |
    ISBN 9780316390415 (v. 8 : pbk.) | ISBN 9780316390422 (v. 9 : pbk.) |
    ISBN 9780316390439 (v. 10 : pbk.) | ISBN 9780316390446 (v. 11 : pbk.) |
    ISBN 9780316390453 (v. 12 : pbk.) | ISBN 9780316390460 (v. 13 : pbk.) |
    ISBN 9780316390484 (v. 14 : pbk.) | ISBN 9780316390491 (v. 15 : pbk.) |
    ISBN 9781975304188 (v. 16 : pbk.) | ISBN 9781975356972 (v. 17 : pbk.) |
    ISBN 9781975356996 (v. 18 : pbk.) | ISBN 9781975357016 (v. 19 : pbk.)
Subjects: CYAC: Science fiction. | BISAC: FICTION / Science Fiction / Adventure.
Classification: pz7.K1755Ain 2014 | DDC [Fic]—dc23
LC record available at https://lccn.loc.gov/2014001175

ISBNs: 978-1-9753-5701-6 (paperback)
       978-1-9753-5702-3 (ebook)

10 9 8 7 6 5 4 3 2 1

LSC-C

Printed in the United States of America

"THIS MIGHT BE A GAME, BUT IT'S NOT SOMETHING YOU PLAY."

—Akihiko Kayaba, *Sword Art Online* programmer

SWORD ART ONLINE moon cradle

Reki Kawahara

abec

bee-pee

Two sets of footsteps echoed through the corridor.

Leading the way through the chalky-white pillars was a girl dressed in gray light armor with dark-brown hair bouncing on her shoulders. A narrow longsword hung at her waist. Just behind her was a juvenile dragon covered in downy pale-yellow hair, its long tail waving. The dragon was just tall enough to see over the girl, though its horns hadn't grown in yet.

The girl's name was Ronie Arabel. The juvenile dragon was Tsukigake.

Based on this heartwarming and beautiful fairy-tale image, it would be hard to imagine that in just a few years, this girl and her dragon would form a partnership as an Integrity Knight and her mount—the strongest battle unit in the entire Underworld.

But in fact, at this early moment, there weren't even a hundred people in the entire world with greater ability in swordplay and sacred arts than Ronie. She had battled at the front line all throughout the dreadful War of the Underworld and the subsequent Rebellion of the Four Empires and had ultimately been promoted to apprentice Integrity Knight—the first in history to be given that honor based entirely on merit.

Despite all that, however, the girl's skill with the blade—sure to flourish further with the training ahead of her—would likely never actually be tested in combat.

After three hundred years of chaos and warfare, true and absolute peace had arrived in the Underworld at last.

Imperials, darklanders, goblins, orcs, ogres, and giants: The six races forged a permanent peace pact. The hierarchy of the four imperial clans and the upper nobles who had been responsible for torturing the common people was scrapped, once and for all. Merchant caravans headed to and fro through the empty space where the Eastern Gate had once stood, and visitors from the Dark Territory came to the capital city of Centoria. The fear and ignorance that had separated the two worlds began to melt away, as surely as the last melting bit of snow in the sun.

The girl ran with her dragon, the light of Solus leaping back and forth across her figure as the line of pillars split it into burning stripes. At her hip, a sword that would never again taste the blood of an enemy swung.

Like this, two sets of footsteps—*tak-tak-tak-tak, plit-plat-plit-plat*—continued into the distance and faded out of earshot.

Seemingly out of nowhere, a large butterfly appeared in her wake, fluttering through the hallway as if enjoying the return of silence.

1

"This way, Ronie!"

She turned and rose on tiptoe, looking in the direction of the voice, and soon saw fiery-red hair bouncing up and down from across the crowd.

Ronie made her way through the mass of arts casters and staff members from Central Cathedral, apologizing all the while. Some of them turned to her in annoyance, but they all leaped back out of the way in alarm when they noticed Tsukigake running behind her.

Only when she finally slipped through to the very front did Ronie exhale in relief.

"You're so late! It's about to start!" her red-haired friend fumed, cheeks puffing with indignation.

"I'm sorry," Ronie apologized one last time. "I just couldn't pick out what to wear..."

"You couldn't pick out...? You're wearing the same thing you always do!" Tiese Schtrinen exclaimed in disbelief.

Like Ronie, Tiese was an apprentice Integrity Knight. Her glinting maple-red eyes were close in tint to her hair, and she wore a navy-blue skirt and a cute printed top that hugged her slender torso. A red leather scabbard hung from her waist, but even that was more like an accessory to complete her outfit.

Ronie realized with regret that she should have worn the southern-made shawl she'd bought last week. On the other side of her friend, Tiese's own dragon, Shimosaki, was rubbing snouts with Tsukigake. Nearby, a young man was watching the display with a gentle smile.

His appearance was closer to a boy than a man, but on his sword belt was quite an impressive longsword, as well as two throwing blades that were bent in the middle. The priority level exuding from the sword was considerable, but it was nothing compared to the throwing weapons. They looked as thin as paper, but they were divine weapons, a class of item that could be found only in tiny numbers throughout the entire world.

Ronie raised her right fist level to her chest and placed her left hand on the hilt of her sword, the formal knight's salute. "Good morning, Sir Renly."

The Integrity Knight Renly Synthesis Twenty-Seven smiled awkwardly at them over the heads of the dragons. "Good morning, Ronie...You don't have to be so stuffy today. It's a festival, after all."

"You call this...a festival?" she wondered. It was February 17th of the year 382 of the Human Era, a perfectly ordinary day on the calendar. There wasn't a single sentence about any celebrations on this day in either the Basic Human Law issued last year or the Taboo Index, which was presently under modification.

But a look around the spacious front plaza of Central Cathedral revealed a crowd that was so large, it might have contained the entire faculty of the tower. Everyone was in a celebratory mood, holding drinks and snacking on food.

Also, the front gate of the cathedral, which was typically closed tight, was open to the people of the capital today. Impromptu standing spaces designated along the inside of the gate were packed with a crowd of at least a thousand onlookers.

"...Yes, I suppose you can't call it anything *but* a festival," Tiese admitted. "But we should probably expect this whenever Kiri... whenever the swordsman delegate does something."

Ronie nodded in agreement. "Of course…I just hope today's events don't knock down the building…"

The three of them glanced toward the plaza—at the center of attention—which was very difficult to describe.

The object was tied down with thin yellow ropes in the middle of the white stone plaza, floating in the block of square-shaped sky a hundred mels to a side and howling eerily as the wind passed by it. The simplest description would be to call it a metallic dragon sculpture.

But as a sign that it wasn't just some art installation, the upper half of its pointed head was made of clear glass. Short wings were attached to either side of its rather long, flat body, and rather than legs, two thick cylinders extended from its enlarged rump. There was no tail.

The object was about five mels in size, standing up so that the cylinders pointed down, and had orange flames licking out of the rump. It was impossible to say exactly *what* it was supposed to be.

…All I can say for certain is that I get a very bad feeling from it, Ronie thought. She tore her eyes from the metal dragon and looked at the three people nearby.

One of them—a young swordswoman with long chestnut-brown hair that rustled in the breeze and a rapier to the left of her pearl-white skirt—turned to Ronie, sensing her eyes. She grinned and raised her right hand to beckon the girl over.

"Go on—she's calling," said Tiese with a grin, prodding Ronie's back. The girl hesitated briefly before summoning her courage and stepping over the yellow rope in front of her. Tsukigake followed her, as always.

Trying to make herself as small as possible, aware that the crowd was watching, Ronie trotted across the open space and came to a stop in front of the swordswoman, giving another crisp and diligent salute.

"Good morning, Swordswoman Subdelegate."

"Good morning, Ronie. Because today is similar to a festival day, you can go ahead and relax a little bit," said the breathtakingly beautiful young woman with a smile. Ronie let the tension in her shoulders ease a little.

"…Yes, Lady Asuna."

"You don't have to do the whole 'Lady' thing, I keep telling you." The other woman pouted. Unfortunately, it was still a very difficult request to oblige.

The woman before her—who looked only a few years older than Ronie—was Asuna, swordswoman subdelegate to the Human Unification Council. And in some ways, she was an even more exalted person than the delegate himself. Every person in the human realm believed that she was the Goddess of Creation Stacia reborn, one of the three goddesses from the world's creation legend.

She herself steadfastly denied being a god in human flesh, but Ronie had witnessed in person, at close range, the sight of Asuna creating a tremendous ravine in the earth with a single swing of her sword during the War of the Underworld. After seeing something like that, calling her anything less than Lady was unthinkable.

If they added a rule to the knighthood's rule book that "no formal address should be recognized," that would settle the matter. But until then, she was going to continue no matter what, and she shook her trembling head to indicate as much. Asuna grimaced awkwardly and changed the subject.

"Anyway, Ronie. I understand that when it comes to sacred arts, you're best with heat elements. Is that right?"

"Y-yes," she answered, surprised. Asuna leaned in closer to whisper.

"In that case, I have a request. Can you commune with the heat elements in there and give me a warning if they're about to go haywire?"

"Wh-what…? Heat elements…in there?" Ronie repeated in confusion, not certain what exactly Asuna was referring to. She looked up at the metallic dragon high above, then noticed two men nearby in an argument.

"...Listen to me, Kiri, my boy. The heat element canisters' life might be capable of theoretically withstanding the heat that is generated, but only if there is an ample supply of frost elements! I know you're not skilled at frost arts, so let me be clear that if the generation of elements stops for even a moment, the whole canister could blow at once!" shouted a whiskered fifty-something man. His words did not mean anything to Ronie, but they sounded dangerous.

Ronie knew this man well; he was Sadore, a metalworker who was said to be the best at his profession in all of Centoria. He'd worked in the city for many years, until he began to assist the knighthood during the Rebellion of the Four Empires, when he was named arsenal master of Central Cathedral.

Across from Master Sadore, looking sullen from the browbeating, was a young man of very average looks, with black hair and eyes.

He was wearing odd gray clothes, like a long-sleeved top with trousers connected to it. There were no weapons at his sides. Brown-gloved hands were clenched behind his head as he argued back at Sadore with annoyance.

"Yeah, yeah, I've heard that so many times, I feel like I've got pester-bugs in my ears. Also, sir, can you stop with the 'Kiri, my boy' thing already?"

"Hmph. I'll never stop. Ever since you brought me that hideously tough branch three years ago and made me ruin six valuable blackbrick grindstones to hone that blade, I swore to myself that I'd call you 'boy' for the rest of eternity."

"*Sheesh*...If I didn't have that sword, the world would be in a terrible state right about now, you know..." Muttering to himself, the young man abruptly spun around and spotted Ronie.

As soon as she saw the big smile break out on that face, which looked as much like a rambunctious child's as it had the day she'd first met him, Ronie felt something clenching her chest, deep down.

She bowed so that if it showed on her face, at least he wouldn't see. "Good morning, Kirito."

She would've called him "Sir," too, but in his case, there really was an official rule against calling him that. So Ronie had no choice but to refer to him as her senior, the way she had when they were both students at the academy.

Kirito had once been an Elite Disciple at the North Centoria Imperial Swordcraft Academy, and now he was the swordsman delegate to the Human Unification Council. He raised a hand to wave and smiled. "Heya, Ronie! How ya doin', Tsukigake?"

Behind Ronie, the juvenile dragon trilled loudly and flapped its tiny wings, then leaped onto Kirito and began to lick his cheeks with abandon. She couldn't help but smile at that.

Then Ronie said to the arsenal master, "Good morning, Master."

"Ah, morning, Miss Ronie," the old man said, his expression instantly morphing into a soft, beaming smile. She scuttled over to him and asked gently, "Um…what was that…heat-canister thing you were talking about?"

"Just what it sounds like. Look at the rump of Dragoncraft Prototype Unit One up there."

"Dragon…craft?" she repeated. It was clear from context that he was referring to the metallic dragon standing before them.

It felt strange for her to refer to this lifeless creation as a dragon. Upon closer examination, the odd whistling sound seemed to be coming from the elliptical rear of the object.

"There are two containers crafted from western adamantium in there, and each one has ten whole heat elements trapped inside of it."

"Wh-what?!" Ronie yelped, shocked. Of the eight different elements that made up sacred arts, heat was the most tempestuous. Unlike frost or wind elements, which could be contained safely for quite a while, heat elements would quickly exude their heat and light and burn up in mere moments. The very first lesson that any child studying sacred arts learned was that if you summoned a heat element, you *had* to focus on it until you applied or unleashed its power.

"B-but…I know adamantium is supposed to be highly heat resistant, but wouldn't being exposed to ten whole heat elements at once cause it to eventually melt and explode…?"

"That's where the trick comes in. On the exterior of the container, we run pipes made of Jorund-giant-centipede shell, which is highly frost resistant. Those pipes are hooked to frost canisters that supply a steady stream of cold that is designed to prevent the heat canisters from melting down, see."

"……Uh…huh……"

It was hard for Ronie to appreciate the "trick," because to her, heat and frost elements were the building blocks of godly sacred arts—a far cry from the crafting of metal and carapace that blacksmiths and craftspeople performed. She had never once considered the concept of combining those two very different things.

"……And is that…going to work…?" she murmured in shock.

Sadore's burly arms spread to his sides in a shrug. "I don't know."

"What?!"

"I'm not the one riding in it—the boy is."

"Whaaaat?!"

What does he mean, "riding in it"? She lifted her face toward the looming dragoncraft, almost afraid of what she would see.

Then she noticed, in the part of the pointed head beneath the clear glass pane, what was inarguably a seat. Metal pipes sprawled and writhed around the seat, and little circular panels were placed here and there with tick marks on them. Thin needles were attached to the center of the panels, twitching and turning with each strange roar the craft produced.

"…D-do you mean…someone's going to sit in there…and release the heat elements…to cause flames to shoot out of the rump canisters…to…"

"To fly, yes. Like a dragon," said Kirito, who had rejoined them.

Nearby, Tsukigake snorted with distaste at the smell of the craft's metal wings.

"Y…y-y-you can't do this!!" she shouted, tugging on the sleeve of Kirito's strange outfit. "If twenty heat elements all go out of control at the same time, it'll rupture this whole thing! Y-you should use wind elements, like the levitating disc in the cathedral."

"Actually, that whole shaft is airtight, which is how there's enough pressure from the wind elements alone to make it work. If you want to fly out in the open air, you need the sheer propulsive power of a heat element's explosion," Kirito said, grinning and looking around. "Plus, look how many people are here to watch. If we try to call it off now, we'll have a second rebellion on our hands."

"Y-you're the one who invited them all to watch!!"

The crowd was here at the Central Cathedral front plaza because Kirito had made a major proclamation that the cathedral's arsenal would be performing a test demonstration for the public.

Now that peace had come to the Underworld, the biggest uproar to be found was whatever the human realm's swordsman delegate was getting up to next. The faculty members and citizens had quite enjoyed the test revival of the northern cave's guardian dragon, so it was only natural for them to be eager about the next experiment.

If Kirito's conversation with the revived dragon had gone any worse than it had, the damage would have been far worse than just a few of the cathedral's trees freezing. Ronie knew how close they had come, and the thought made her lose her balance.

Thankfully, the subdelegate was right behind her to provide stability. Asuna had known Kirito for a long time, apparently, and she said with all-seeing resignation, "There's no point in arguing, Ronie. When he gets this way, you just have to let him go through with it."

"B-but…you can't…Well…I suppose you're right…," Ronie

mourned, pausing in the act of shaking her head to nod it instead. In these few years, Ronie had learned full well that when Kirito had his mind set on something, he was going to do it one way or another.

Well, we might as well do everything we can to avoid a terrible disaster, she thought, focusing on the heart of the dragoncraft.

While she was an apprentice Integrity Knight, Ronie had not yet reached the point of free control over the secret art of the knighthood known as Incarnation. Shortening sacred arts to a minimal length through Incarnation the way that Kirito and the senior knights did was impossible for her, but lately she was getting the knack of sensing the status of generated elements, at least.

Like Master Sadore had said, there were many heat elements trapped inside the dragoncraft. But that didn't mean they were behaving themselves. They shivered and trembled with indignation, pulsating as they awaited their chance to break right through the shell around them.

If they were this unruly in their elemental state, what would happen if they were unleashed? The thought sent a shiver down her spine—but at this point, all she could do was watch and wait.

"Um...I've communed with the heat elements, Lady Asuna. It appears that they are still under control for now," she reported at a murmur.

"Thanks," Asuna whispered back. "Maintain that circuit, then."

"I w-will," Ronie stated, right as she heard Kirito shout from a distance:

"Let's get started, then! Asuna, give me a countdown!"

"Wh-why does it have to be me?!"

"You always did one before we busted into the boss chambers, remember?" Kirito said, which didn't make any sense to Ronie. But Asuna understood and shook her head in disbelief.

She raised her hand and uttered the initiation of a sacred art: "System Call!"

Next, she smoothly built the command for a voice-enlarging art out of wind and crystal elements. Asuna's control over Incarnation was still developing, but as far as practical application of sacred arts went, even the most elite members of the cathedral couldn't hold a candle to her.

Asuna faced the thin funnel-shaped swirl of glass floating in the air and said loudly and clearly, *"Thank you for your patience and interest, everyone! The Central Cathedral arsenal is about to conduct a flight test of Dragoncraft Prototype One!"*

Her magnified voice filled the area, eliciting a roar from the cathedral faculty beyond the ropes and the civilians crowded into the spectator area inside the gate. To the north, the armor of the Integrity Knights gleamed and sparkled in the sun from the large terrace on the thirtieth floor of the building itself.

Amid the applause and cheers, Kirito waved to the onlookers and began to climb the long ladder leading up to the dragoncraft. He reached the head in just seconds, opened part of the clear glass panel, and slid inside.

Kirito sat in the seat that pointed up toward the sky and strapped himself down with strips of leather. There was rather large eyewear hanging around his neck, and he brought it up to wrap around his head. Then he leaned over to look at Sadore down below and pointed his thumb upward.

Sadore retreated to where Ronie and Asuna were standing, then ushered them back another twenty-plus mels. Ronie had to gauge the distance carefully, so as not to lose her connection to the heat elements.

"I will now begin the countdown! Feel free to join in, everyone!" Asuna announced to the crowd, as comfortably as if she were used to doing this. She raised her hands and extended all her fingers.

"Here goes! Ten! Nine! Eight!"

With each number, she folded in a finger, and the throng of thousands added their voices to the chorus. Tiese and Renly were happily joining in, too.

Ronie squeezed Tsukigake around the neck and chanted, "Seven! Six! Five!"

Suddenly, the vibrating of the heat elements increased. Kirito had begun controlling them directly through Incarnation. His astonishing power flowed into Ronie, too, through the elements with which she was communing.

Once again, there was a clenching sensation deep within her chest.

This feeling is the one thing I cannot let leave me. As his page, I have to let it sleep quietly, until the day my life eventually dwindles due to old age.

Ronie could feel her eyes welling up, and she blinked hard, keeping the emotion away from Asuna's attention nearby, as she shouted, "Four! Three! Two!"

Hwirrrrr! The roaring of the dragoncraft grew louder and louder. The shining silver object began to shudder, and the light coming from the tubes at its base changed from red to orange to yellow.

"One…Zero!!" the crowd cheered, shaking the cobblestones. Kirito's voice could be heard distantly shouting, "Discharge!!"

That was the word to release the power of the elements.

At once, twenty heat elements burst, releasing the power they contained. There was a tremendous blast, and white flames shot from the rear of the dragoncraft. It burned the white marble stone that supposedly held near-infinite life to the point of turning red, sending up plumes of bright smoke. The crowd buzzed with alarm.

And through all that smoke, the metal dragon shot upward like a silver arrow.

The sky was full of a high-pitched tearing sound the likes of which Ronie had never heard before. Jets of fire were roaring from the two tubes as the dragoncraft soared higher and higher into the air.

The ferocity of the unleashed heat elements was so great that when Ronie held her palms out, the sensation stung her skin.

Ordinarily, any container holding that kind of phenomenal heat would lose its life value instantly, melting or burning away. The dragoncraft *should* have exploded. But because the narrow piping embedded around the canisters was pumping ultracold frost elements through at all times, the heat was contained. As a result, the incredible power of the heat elements was funneled directly toward the open end of the tubes, pushing the huge dragoncraft straight upward.

For the first time in the history of the Underworld, a person was flying through the sky on something other than a dragon.

"……It's incredible…"

Tears appeared in Ronie's eyes for a different reason than they had moments earlier.

Through her blotted vision, the silver dragoncraft shot up and up, seemingly cresting beyond even the top of Central Cathedral.

If the dragoncraft stayed in one spot on the ground, the requirements to generate endless frost elements would quickly sap all the spatial sacred resources nearby, but moving at high speed meant the craft would consistently be traveling just fast enough to stay within an adequate supply of fresh new resources. That meant that—hypothetically—the man-made dragon could reach heights that even an ordinary dragon could not approach.

At last, Ronie felt as though she understood the true intention of the swordsman delegate. Kirito wasn't just trying to get that thing to fly—he might be trying to use it to cross the obstacle that no living thing could surpass: the Wall at the End of the World…

But no sooner had the thought occurred to Ronie than she sensed the heat elements expanding.

The canisters were beginning to warp. The heat was melting them. For whatever reason, the supply of frost elements meant to keep the metal's temperature low had stalled.

"Ah! Lady Asuna! The heat elements—," she cried, but then there was an ugly sound from above—*bowumm!*—and black smoke began to issue from one of the thruster tubes.

The dragoncraft abruptly entered a rotational spin as it rose.

The course of the object drifted southward—right toward the wall of Central Cathedral, around the ninety-fifth floor.

"It's going to hit!!" screamed Ronie, clutching her hands to her chest. The crowd shrieked with alarm.

Shang!! Asuna drew the rapier from the sheath at her side. She pointed the breathtaking blade, shining with Solus's rainbow light, straight at the cathedral above.

"...Okeydoke!" she cried, which did not sound like the sort of thing a god would say, and she waved the tip of the sword to the left.

As though she'd just dragged it herself, the ninety-fifth floor and those above it in the enormous Central Cathedral shifted loudly and heavily to the west.

In the span of a single moment, the dragoncraft shot through the space this created, black smoke trailing behind it.

There was a bright flash in the sky far to the south.

Then came the explosion.

Although some of the power had no doubt been expended in the upward flight of the dragoncraft, the simultaneous eruption of twenty heat elements was nonetheless a tremendous thing to behold.

Because elements could ordinarily be controlled by only one finger at a time, even the greatest of casters could manage to generate and maintain only ten elements at once. According to stories, the head of the senate that had once controlled the Axiom Church could also use his toes, for a total of twenty elements. The late pontifex, Administrator, could even use the ends of her hair as terminal points, giving her command of nearly a hundred elements at once—but of course, Ronie had never seen those things for herself.

If that was true for a knight like Ronie, then the civilians who had packed themselves into the cathedral were understandably shocked. An orange light like a second Solus flashed high above, and an earth-trembling roar hit their ears as nearly the entire crowd lifted up their arms to cover their heads.

Of course, it was only unprocessed heat elements bursting high up in the air, so despite the eye-popping light and sound, there was no actual damage to the people hundreds of mels below on the ground.

The onlookers slowly looked back up and saw thick black smoke puffing outward, hiding the top of the cathedral, which had slid back into its rightful place.

The explosion had been several times the size of the fireworks that had been shot off to celebrate the new year two months earlier. Everyone must have wondered what had happened to the swordsman delegate who was riding that steel dragon. Ronie was one of them, of course, and she watched wide-eyed, with her hands clutched before her breast.

"K—!"

She was about to shout his name when Asuna tapped her on the shoulder.

"He's all right," the other girl said, without a hint of worry, just as a small shape plummeted right through the bottom of the thick black smoke cloud.

It was a person. All the material making up the dragoncraft had evaporated into spatial sacred resources, but there wasn't a single visible burn mark on the dark clothing of the figure who spun and tumbled downward.

The silhouette spread its arms. The fabric of the sleeves seemed to melt behind it, forming thin wings that extended directly from the shoulders. Those dragon-like wings beat a few times, slowing the figure's descent until it eventually came to a standstill in the air.

It appeared to be the sacred art of flying, thought to be lost forever with the death of the pontifex. But in fact, this was not an art. He had overwritten the ways of the world entirely, using Incarnation to transform the material of his clothes into actual wings and turn himself into a living being capable of flight.

There was no other human being in existence who could achieve this feat. A murmur rippled through the watching crowd, and it quickly turned into a tremendous storm of applause.

The dragoncraft flight test, which had been the purpose of this event, had largely been a failure, but Kirito smiled and waved as he slowly descended toward the ground. Ronie found herself clapping wildly at the sight of him, too. Kirito's ability to put preposterous ideas into motion and achieve preposterous results had not changed in the years she had known him.

Despite the fact that she was smiling, Ronie could sense liquid pooling at the edges of her eyes. She clenched her eyelids shut and wiped the tears away, making a silent prayer for no one's ears but her own.

If possible, I hope that these days can last for eternity.

2

The vast space on the fiftieth floor of Central Cathedral, known as the Great Hall of Ghostly Light, was now the meeting space of the Human Unification Council.

In the center of the floor, where there had once been nothing but polished marble stone, there was now a mammoth round table carved from an ancient platinum oak, surrounded by twenty chairs.

Seated in one of them, his shoulders hunched with mortification, was Kirito. A large man stood over him, bellowing in a voice like thunder.

"Now, Swordsman Delegate, I'm going to let you hear it for good this time!!"

"......Yes, sir."

"I will *not* be destroying anything this time—you swore upon your swords! I presume you haven't forgotten saying *that*!!"

".........No, sir."

The greatest swordsman in the entire human realm was being scolded like a student, and playing the role of teacher was a knight wearing a suit of deep-red bronze armor. His face was stern and imposing, and his short hair and sharp eyes were the color of flames. That was Deusolbert Synthesis Seven, one of the most senior Integrity Knights.

"If Lady Asuna had not made use of her godly power, the ninety-fifth floor of the cathedral would be completely burned out at this moment! I don't care if it is uninhabited now—think of how the people of the city would lament if the historic, symbolic white tower became known as the Charred Tower! It seems to me that you are utterly unaware of the status you possess! Leave the finer issues of developing arts and tools to the arts masters and blacksmiths who make it their calling!"

Another knight, sitting a slight distance away at the table, cut off Deusolbert's lecture before it went on forever. "That's enough for now, Deusolbert. Look at the swordsman delegate—he's as wilted as a slug-bug in the sun."

Her luscious voice, containing more than a hint of mirth, accompanied armor polished to a mirrorlike shine and flowing black hair that hung down her back. A longsword with a platinum hilt rested on her left hip, and cradled in her right arm was a baby with a shade of dark-blue hair that was rare in the human realm.

"But, Commander..."

"It wouldn't do to scold the delegate so much that he runs away from home again. We've got the meeting with the Dark Territory next month, after all."

The smiling woman, as beautiful and graceful as a flower, was the commander of the Integrity Knights, Fanatio Synthesis Two. She was the second commander in the knighthood's history and possessed the greatest swordsmanship in the world, but you wouldn't know it from the way she gently cradled the sleeping infant.

Fanatio looked over to the deflated young man, a smile glowing on her face, and said, "So you'll have to behave yourself for a little while, boy."

Kirito looked up, wearing a big, awkward grimace. "It's much scarier when you call me 'boy' rather than 'delegate.'"

"Ha-ha. Wouldn't you say that your fear is an admission of guilt coming from within?" Fanatio said, side-eyeing Asuna

the subdelegate, who stood nearby with her arms folded. Asuna was smiling, but her eyes were not; in fact, they seemed to be twitching.

Fanatio then looked to Ronie, who stood beside a pillar not far from the table. For some reason, Fanatio's smile seemed a bit impish. But the mischievous look quickly vanished, and she patted Kirito on the shoulder.

"The important thing is that there was no real damage once again, so I suppose we can leave your scolding at that. Instead, I will merely insist that you spend the rest of the day until dinnertime tending to your office work."

"……All right," Kirito murmured in resignation. Fanatio grabbed his shoulders while he was still seated and pushed him toward the table before beckoning toward Ronie. The girl rushed over to receive the baby.

"Would you mind watching Berche for a bit, Ronie? Lately, whenever I let him play by himself, he winds up destroying things."

"Y-yes, I'd be happy to!" Ronie said, holding out her arms. The knight commander then handed her the sleeping baby. The apprentice was stunned by the sudden increase in weight. As a knight in training, Ronie could easily swing a standard-issue two-mel greatsword with a single hand, but the weight of a child was something else entirely.

She gingerly rebalanced her arms, eliciting a sleepy murmur from the one-year-old boy, though it wasn't quite enough to wake him up. She bowed briefly to Fanatio and returned to the pillar. Tsukigake greeted her there, extending its snout to sniff curiously at the baby.

At the round table, Kirito, Asuna, Fanatio, and Deusolbert were joined by the leader of the sacred artificers brigade—the group that had previously been known as priests or monks—and other senior cathedral officials seated here and there as the meeting came to order.

"Let's start with the reopening of the southern cave in the End Mountains, as reported on earlier…"

"Digging out the cave should be possible, but the bigger problem will be constructing a road that runs through the dense jungles of the south…"

This wasn't a formal council meeting, so as an apprentice, Ronie wasn't required to be present. Her partner, Tiese, for instance, was in the great library studying the sacred arts formulas she found so difficult.

But there was something Ronie wanted to ask Kirito about in secret. She wanted to know the truth about a fleeting mental image she'd captured while watching the flight test earlier that morning. And if you took your eye off Kirito for even a moment, he would disappear to some other location in the cathedral or the shopping district of Centoria—or even fly himself to some other city or town in the realm—so she needed to catch him when the meeting was over, before he could vanish.

During Incarnation training, they sometimes forced the trainees to balance atop a narrow metal pillar on one foot for hours at a time, so resting against a pillar and waiting for the meeting to end was no issue at all. Her dragon was better behaved than Tiese's, so, at the very least, she didn't have to worry that it would attempt to sharpen its teeth on the stone out of boredom.

As she stood there, listening to the lively debate at the table, there came an adorable sneeze from the baby in her arms. He didn't wake up, but she worried that he might be cold, so she walked over to the window, where the rays of Solus peeked in. His dark-blue hair sparkled in the sunlight, and the sight of those innocent chubby cheeks caused Ronie's breath to catch in her throat.

A baby…, she thought, grinning.

Her mind traveled back to last month, when she'd returned home to the north side of the capital. Those memories were not nearly so enjoyable.

The Arabel family had originally been a sixth-ranked noble house under the old peerage system.

They hadn't led a wealthy, extravagant life. They hadn't owned their own estate like the higher nobles, and their only income had been the salary of her father's job as a platoon leader of the Imperial Guard and a small noble allowance. It had been far from the vast sums of tax money that first- and second-ranked nobles had received every month without working, and it hadn't even measured up to the income of the successful merchants who did business in the central district of Centoria.

Still, she had an enjoyable time, living with her bright and fastidious mother, stern but gentle father, and her scamp of a little brother.

The one thing that wore on her spirits was the parties that her father's fourth-ranked family threw every now and then. He was the fourth son, and though Ronie's grandfather passed away when she was just a baby, the first son, who became the patriarch—Ronie's uncle—held an attitude that he and his family were proud nobles and were above it all. Ronie's fanciful aunt wore an expression of unbridled disgust whenever social custom required her to compliment Ronie's mother on her old, faded dress, and the daughter often threw a fit and sulked when it came time to go to another party.

But after the quashing of the Rebellion of the Four Empires, the peerage system was revolutionized. All the estates were released, and nobles were no longer separated into ranks. The noble allowances remained for a short while afterward, but they weren't enough to live on, so all nobles were forced to find employment in the newly re-formed human army.

For the great noble houses, this was nothing short of a profound transformation, but from Ronie's point of view, it was simply putting them back in the place where they belonged. The time when a person's family name earned them fancy titles like *general* or *strategist* was over. Only those who were recognized for their actual skill, intelligence, and experience were placed in positions of importance.

In other words, at present, all the noble families were on the same level.

But there were a few minor exceptions to this rule. And out of all the noble families in Centoria, they happened to be the families of Ronie Arabel and Tiese Schtrinen, the two people chosen to be apprentice Integrity Knights.

Last month, Ronie had gone back home for the first time since being made an apprentice. Her parents and brother were doing well, especially her brother, who was now a student at the North Centoria Imperial Swordcraft Academy. He was excited to see her and tried to swing her sword (he couldn't even draw it from its sheath) and challenge her at arm wrestling (he couldn't push her wrist half a cen) and so on. Her father wanted to ask all about life at the cathedral, and her mother's cooking was as delicious as ever. It was a wonderful evening...

But the next day, her three uncles and their families barged in, and to her surprise, they brought many gifts:

Marriage proposals for Ronie, that was.

The Integrity Knights, of which Ronie would one day be a full-fledged member, were the protectors of the Axiom Church under the old regime and were the objects of overwhelming fear and reverence for the entire population. That situation had not changed much now that the Church had been revamped into the Human Unification Council. If anything, the fact that many Integrity Knights had lost their lives in the War of the Underworld only made them more heroic in the public eye.

If they could marry one of those knights into their family, their rank and income would increase exponentially, her uncles and aunts seemed to think. Families with sons of appropriate age offered them as prizes. If there were no sons, heirs of close relatives would be offered instead. The number of personal-identification papers they had gathered to present to her for the purpose of making their offerings look better was impressive indeed.

"Apprentice knight or not, a woman's most important duty is the

bearing and raising of children. Even the commander of the Integrity Knights gave birth to a baby boy! So there can't be any law that says you can't do the same, my girl. Look here, I recommend my son." "No, mine is better!" "But you haven't seen our boy yet..."

Long ago, Kirito had let Ronie and Tiese in on a secret. The pontifex who had ruled the old Axiom Church had found the most skilled individuals in swordsmanship and sacred arts from all over the country and molded them into Integrity Knights. In reality, that meant performing a forbidden process called the Synthesis Ritual, which removed all their old memories and implanted a false one. According to this false memory, they were not human beings, but knights summoned to the mortal plane from the celestial realm.

It was a dreadful, terrible thing to do—but in the presence of her aunts and uncles, Ronie couldn't help but begrudgingly admit the logical brilliance of how it had set up the operation of the knighthood.

She resisted the urge to perform the sacred art of creating a smoke screen and running away and, instead, explained to her relatives that an Integrity Knight in the family would not bring greater noble holdings or estates. But they refused to believe her, to the point that they accused her of living in the lap of luxury within the cathedral, at which point her father flew into a rage and drove them out of the house.

But although she thanked her father, she couldn't shake the thought.

He always said that she should be with the man she *wanted* to marry, but surely he must be dying to have grandchildren already. And more important than that, her parents had to be worried sick about her being in the Integrity Knighthood. If war hadn't broken out, Ronie would have graduated from Swordcraft Academy, taken on the second or third son of some other noble family as a husband, and continued the Arabel family name.

So it was clear that they hoped she would get married and start a family sooner rather than later. And for her part, she wanted to make that come true so they'd know that her future was secure.

But after she left and returned to Central Cathedral, Ronie found herself silently apologizing to them over and over.

I'm sorry, Father. I'm sorry, Mother. I'm pretty sure—quite sure, in fact—that I'll never be married or have children in my life.

Because I'll never be with the one I truly love.

Ronie was broken out of her reminiscence when little Berche woke up and started to stir in her arms. In a panic, she awkwardly tried to lull him, but the baby showed no signs of calming down any time soon.

"It's all right. There, there. Who's a good boy?" she cooed as the baby's face got redder and redder. Just as it scrunched up, and Berche prepared to burst into tears, a hand reached out and grabbed the baby by his clothes.

"It's going to take more than that, trust me," said his mother, Commander Fanatio. Her benevolent smile and beautiful features were framed by flowing black hair.

"Here we go! Look, you're flying!" she said, tossing little Berche into the air. It looked as easy as a flick of the wrist, but this *was* the strongest of the Integrity Knights, after all.

The infant flipped and spun higher and higher toward the soaring ceiling of the Great Hall of Ghostly Light.

"Wha—? Fana…L-look out…!!" yelped Ronie, freezing awkwardly. The boy's upward momentum petered out just before his head touched the map of the celestial realm on the ceiling, and he began to fall straight down. When he plopped back into his mother's arms, he immediately giggled and cackled with excitement.

"I can't imagine how I'm going to deal with him. Thank you for looking after him, Ronie. I'll have to ask you for help again in the future," Fanatio said, favoring her with a smile and heading for the exit. Deusolbert and the other leaders followed her; the meeting had adjourned.

"Seems like part of the problem is *how* she's raising him...," muttered a voice in the background. Ronie turned to see Kirito, his expression a mixture of exasperation and fear. Next to him, Asuna was making an awkward face as well.

"W-well, one day he's going to be a knight and ride on a dragon, s-so...it's probably good for him to get used to heights at a young age."

"Between Sheyta's baby and him, the future's going to be a real disast...um, a real delight," Kirito went on, shaking his head and putting his hands on his hips. "And now that my work is done for the day, I'll go check on Unit Two..."

"Wh-what?! You've already got another one?!"

"Yeah, and this one's amazing. Between the heat-element engine and thrusters, there's a wind-element compressor, which makes it possible to engage in turbo—"

"Maybe instead of focusing on power, Kirito, you should do something about its safety!"

Ronie just barely had the willpower to thrust herself between the Black Swordsman and his divine partner, who spoke in the unfamiliar sacred tongue considerably more than the average person. "Um, ex...excuse me, Kirito..."

"Yeah?"

"Um, I wanted to talk...Ah, well, I wanted to ask you something, actually..."

Kirito's black eyes blinked at her, but he quickly favored her with a friendly grin. "Yeah, of course. I suppose we can have an early teatime. What about you, Asuna?"

He looked over at the swordswoman subdelegate, who was murmuring to herself. "Well, I'd like to join you, but I'm supposed to be attending a lecture on sacred arts at the Great Library after this."

"Ah, I see. Well, the second scribe *is* intimidating, I'll admit. Better not be late," Kirito said with a visible shiver.

"Only to students performing poorly, perhaps." Asuna smiled. She took a step back and turned to Ronie. "Well, I'll see you at dinner, then. Ronie, make sure that Kirito doesn't fill up on sweets."

"I…I will!" she said, bowing, as Kirito grumbled about being treated like a child. Asuna waved and turned to stride away, leaving a rainbow-tinged afterimage behind her. Kirito watched her go through the large doors to the south, then looked back at Ronie.

"So…I guess we could go up to the eightieth floor or so. I sure could go for some snowplum cake right about now…"

"I'll have the kitchen staff prepare some for you."

"Get me two…no, three slices! I'll see you up there!" Kirito said without giving Ronie any time to interject, and he raced through the north door to the levitation shaft.

She reached out to stroke the neck of Tsukigake, who was finally nodding off to sleep, and murmured, "I should probably just bring the whole cake…"

In the kitchen on the tenth floor, Ronie took an entire cake with sugar-frosted snowplums on top—much to the disapproving stare of the chef—put it in a basket with a portable teakettle, and headed for the eightieth floor of the cathedral.

When she stepped on the elevating platform, it rose on its own. It had once been operated by a person, but now that it was automatic, that girl had been relieved of duty. From what Ronie had heard, she had taken on a new career in the arsenal in recognition of her excellent skill with wind arts.

Like its informal name of Cloudtop Garden suggested, the eightieth floor of Central Cathedral was covered in flowers, despite being indoors. Atop a small and gentle hill in the center of the spacious meadow covered in silver frostlilies stood the swordsman delegate, dressed in black.

Kirito had his hand against the young osmanthus tree planted in the middle of the hilltop. As Ronie approached, he turned and grinned at her.

"Hi. Thanks."

"This is one of the duties of a page, after all." She giggled and spread out a cloth. Then she took plates out of the basket, as well as the large, pre-sliced cake, much to Kirito's childlike delight. She plated slices for herself, Tsukigake, and Kirito; poured out two cups of tea; and told him to dig in.

"Thanks, this looks great!" Kirito said, beginning to eat quickly, as though he were in a competition with the dragon. Ronie felt a warmth spreading through her chest as she watched him go.

When she had opportunities to be alone with Kirito these days, she felt both a sense of bliss and a deep longing for her wish to come true. If only there were a sacred art of time-freezing...If only she could live within this moment for all eternity...

But of course, no sacred arts command could control the flow of time. It never moved backward and never stopped, but continued flowing toward the future at the same steady rate.

It was because of time's eternal flux that the world had survived its greatest peril and arrived at the peace it now enjoyed. Someday, Ronie would be made a full-fledged Integrity Knight and soar across the skies on the back of a grown-up Tsukigake. Part of her looked forward to that, of course. But she couldn't stop herself from wishing, *Please, Time, just stop.*

"...nie. Ronie?"

Kirito's voice startled her out of her gentle reverie.

"Oh, s-sorry! Did you want more?"

"No. I mean, yes...but that wasn't what I was saying." Kirito held out his empty plate to her. "Weren't you going to ask me something?"

"Ah..."

At last, she remembered why she was here in the first place. "I'm sorry!" Ronie stammered. "That's right...Um, it was about that steel dragon you created...the dragoncraft."

Kirito took a big bite out of the second slice of cake she offered him and nodded. "Uh-huh."

"Um, well, I was thinking...er, actually, I was worried that..."

She looked left and right before continuing in hushed tones, "You might be planning to use that dragoncraft...to fly over the Wall at the End—?"

Kirito suddenly let out a muffled gurgle, thumped at his chest with one hand, and scrabbled in the empty air with the other. Ronie hastily handed him his cup of tea, which he downed all at once before exhaling.

The black-haired young man smiled the same way he had when she'd first met him—like a mischievous young boy who knew exactly what he was getting himself into.

"I should have figured that my page would know me that well. I can't hide anything from you."

"What? Th-then it's true?"

"Yeah, pretty much," he admitted, scratching at his cheek as though it were no big deal. Ronie stared at him in disbelief.

The Wall at the End of the World. That was the common name for the barrier that spanned the perimeter around both the human realm and the dark realm—the Underworld as a whole. Its height seemed to be endless, in fact.

From Centoria, it simply blended into the blue of the sky, hiding its existence from the residents, but Ronie had seen it with her own eyes just one time. It was when she had joined Kirito on a visit to the mountain goblins' domain in the far north of the Dark Territory. It had taken her breath away when she'd noticed the faded, distant cliff over the horizon.

According to the goblins, the wall was made not of earth but of some ultra-hard mineral. They had difficulty even chiseling a tiny hole in it, much less carving caves or stairs into its surface. In three hundred years of history, every last foolhardy attempt to scale it had ended in death.

The giants and ogres had similar tales about the wall, making it clear that there was a common understanding shared by the peoples of the Dark Territory: The wall was completely impassable and literally represented the end of the world.

Or so we thought.

"So, um, well," Ronie stammered, trying to regain her footing. She had an inkling of what his intentions were, but she didn't expect him to admit it so easily. She took a sip of tea to steady herself. "Um…So does that mean you've already tested whether you can cross the wall with your flying arts?"

"Yep," Kirito said, but he soon shook his head. "I tried it and gave up. Couldn't even get over it with wings made of Incarnation, much less flight with wind elements. Seems like getting to a certain fixed height increases gravity to a nearly unlimited level…"

He leaned back against the osmanthus tree, arms folded, muttering more to himself than to her.

"…But when I threw a knife straight up from that theoretical elevation limit, it went much, much higher. Meaning that the limit doesn't completely block *all* objects. I think it selectively blocks humanoids. Growing wings doesn't change my unit ID, after all… So the only option I have is to gamble that by completely sealing myself inside a movable shell, the system itself will recognize the shell as a nonliving object, allowing me to pass…"

At this point, Ronie was completely lost. She raised a hand. "Um, are you saying that you can't cross the wall in your own body, but if you ride that metal dragon, you might be able to get over it?"

"Huh…?" Kirito looked up at last, blinking repeatedly. "Ah, sorry. Right, yes, that's correct. The truth is, I've already tried flying paper or leather airplanes—er, dragons—with sacred arts and Incarnation. But it didn't work…If I'm moving them myself, it seems to treat them like clothes or armor. The dragon has to be able to fly on its own. But if it's going to withstand the temperature of heat elements, it needs to be made of metal, and it needs power to be able to push all that weight, which means more heat elements, and it's just a vicious cycle, you see…"

"Wow…that all sounds very complicated…," Ronie murmured, falling into the same swamp of thought that was plaguing Kirito before she came back to her senses. "Oh, I mean, not that! I wanted to ask you about something else…"

"Hmm? What?"

"*Why* do you need to go over the wall? I was your page for a long time, so I understand your instinct to want to overcome any obstacle you're faced with...but I feel as though there are...more important things to focus on now..."

She started off strong but soon realized that it was beginning to sound like a lecture, and she felt ashamed. Kirito clapped her on the shoulder.

"Thanks, Ronie. I feel bad for making you worry all the time," he said with a smile, which caused her heart to skip a beat. She quickly suppressed her emotions. Kirito didn't seem to recognize the effect he had on her, though. He put his hands behind his head and looked up into the sky.

"...But the truth is, I happen to think that getting over that wall is actually the highest priority in all of the Underworld right now."

"Um...what does that mean?"

"...Listen, don't tell anyone else. Not even Tiese or Fanatio."

She was surprised by his sudden demand but agreed all the same. The real shock was what Kirito said next, however.

"At this rate, there's going to be another war."

"......!! N-no, that can't be...! We finally reached an era of peace..."

Kirito shook his head, his expression stern. "I'm afraid that's not going to last very long...The Eastern Gate collapsed, trading began between the two worlds, and tourists have come in great numbers from the Dark Territory. For now, they are enjoying sights and foods that are rare and exotic to them. But eventually, they won't be able to help but notice the definitive difference between the two worlds."

"Difference...?"

"Yes. The human realm is far too rich in resources, and the dark realm is far too poor. You saw that red sky and the dark-black charcoal...The land around Obsidia was the only place that was reasonably lush, but the demi-humans have no claim to that place—it's run by humans. Slowly but surely, unrest will build among the goblins, orcs, and giants. Asuna and I tried to do what we could to make their lands more fertile, but nothing worked. The spatial resources…the sacred power just isn't there."

She listened to him, not speaking a word. *Yes, the sight of the barren land of the Dark Territory is seared into my mind. But until this moment, I always just assumed that was the way it was meant to be. I never entertained the idea of actually doing something about it.*

"Kirito…I…," she murmured.

He looked at her with those deep-black eyes and smiled gently. "I'm sorry—I'm not criticizing you. Nobody can help it; that's just how the Underworld was built to begin with. It was designed for war to happen between the starved dark realm and the rich human realm. War *did* break out, and many lives were lost. All we managed to do was avoid the worst possible ending. So for the sake of those who did die, we have to make sure that history doesn't repeat itself."

"B-but, what should we…?"

"There's only one answer. The demi-humans need land they can be proud of—something more than the distant wastes that humans drove them to. They need real countries of their own, where they don't have to be the '*non*humans.'"

"Real…countries."

She'd been having trouble following anything Kirito was saying in this conversation, but that phrase was the one thing she understood instinctively.

The territory of the mountain goblins was the only demi-human land that Ronie had seen for herself. Their country was in the hilly region far to the northeast of where the Eastern Gate had once stood. No wheat grew from their ground, and no fish swam in their rivers. It was literally a barren wasteland.

Their previous two generations of chieftains, Hagashi and Kosogi, had both died in the war, and they had only just gotten a new leader, so the tribe was stagnant and slow to recover. In the old days when power was law, the giants, orcs, or maybe even the flatland goblins would have wiped them out by now.

When Ronie had accompanied Kirito on the trip to their land, the sight of the enfeebled and abandoned on crude straw mats as well as starving children whimpering in the dirt had left her speechless. The large stock of supplies they'd brought from the human realm helped avoid an utter collapse, but it was no more than a short-term solution to a long-term crisis. The soil there simply wasn't capable of supporting the multiplying population of goblins.

But before this point, Ronie had never given it a second thought. If anything, she'd tried to forget about it. She'd tried to forget the sight of goblin children snatching from her hands the hard-baked bread renowned for its long-lasting texture and certainly not its flavor. The enthusiasm with which they had wolfed it down was enough to make the simple bread seem like a feast fit for a king.

Supplies were still being sent out regularly from the human realm, as far as she was aware. She'd told herself that this was enough, and she'd turned a blind eye to the fact that she'd lived a life of comfort and luxury as a human noble, even if she was a lower one.

But when Kirito had mentioned "real countries," Ronie couldn't help but face the hard truth. That wasteland was no country at all—it wasn't even true territory. That was a land of exile. It was a place of punishment, not of habitation.

"......Kirito...I......I..."

Ronie hung her head. Her fork clanked onto the plate bearing her half-eaten cake. *Nobles have a duty far greater than the privileges they are granted. They must fight at all times for the sake of the powerless. In the sacred tongue, this is called "noblesse oblige."*

Two years ago, when she was an ignorant primary trainee at the academy, it was Kirito who had taught her this.

And somehow, I let myself forget...In fact, I never thought of the goblins as fellow humans to begin with. I pitied their plight, but a part of me thought it was just their fate in life to suffer this way...

A tear welled up and dripped from her eye onto the white plate. Tsukigake trilled with concern, and a hand reached over and rubbed Ronie's head.

"I'm sorry, Ronie. I knew that talking about this might might upset you," Kirito murmured softly. "But...you don't have to be so hard on yourself. We're able to send supplies to the dark realm because we reined in the extravagance of the emperors and nobles, and we rebuilt the human realm really quickly. Neither of those things would have happened without your hard work. So the truth is, you've been doing your part to help them already."

"Do you...really think that?"

"I do. I've been to the mountain goblins' land since then, and the children you gave bread to still remembered you."

More tears trickled down her cheeks, for a slightly different reason this time. He reached out with a simple handkerchief to wipe them away. She had to fight the urge to leap into his arms, bury her face against his chest, and weep. Instead, she let her head hang until the tears stopped, then lifted her face and smiled.

"...Thank you. I'm fine now...I'm sorry for crying in the middle of our conversation."

"I knew you were a crybaby since your first year at the academy, Ronie," Kirito reassured her with a grin. She made a face and glared at him, but there was another round of painful needling deep in her heart that she had to endure.

She swallowed more tea and blinked the remaining tears away. "Um...I think I understand your thoughts on the matter now. The goblins and orcs need beautiful, fertile lands just like in the human realm. If there's no place like that in the Underworld, we'll have to go beyond the End of the World. And the first step to doing that is getting past the wall with that dragoncraft... Is that correct?"

"You got it...But I bet that the real hard part comes after crossing the wall...," Kirito admitted, bobbing his head.

"But," she asked hesitantly, "is there really another side beyond the wall? What if it simply continues forever and ever...?"

"I've considered that. But the thing is…if that wall really is the end of this world, I don't think there's any need for it to be a wall at all. It would simply be an impenetrable address…Something like a void."

"A void…Like some invisible space that can't be traversed?"

"That's right. But the Wall at the End of the World is an actual, physical wall—an extremely tall and tough one, that's all. What if the reason for that is to keep the residents of the world from facing some phenomenon they're not prepared to understand…? It's possible that the end of the world will no longer be the end once you've gotten there…Though it all depends on how much spare power and space the Main Visualizer has, of course…"

Ronie frowned. He was going off on one of his impossible tangents again. Kirito realized it, too, and scratched his head apologetically.

"Sorry, when I'm talking with you, I seem to have a habit of just saying whatever's in my head. Let's see…How about this? The fact is, there's no end to the world."

"No…end…?"

Again, it was an unfamiliar concept to Ronie. She'd been born and raised in North Centoria, so the first "end of the world" she'd known was the Everlasting Walls that split the Centoria into four wedge-shaped segments. But then she'd learned that the Norlangarth Empire extended far to the north beyond those walls. Specifically, that it, along with the three other empires of similar shape, composed the entirety of the human realm, which took the form of a circle.

It wasn't until she started at the youth training academy at age eight that she was taught about the frightening Dark Territory that existed in the space beyond the End Mountains, which surrounded the circular realm. But her teacher did not tell her any specifics about the dark realm—looking back, she doubted the teacher even knew—so it wasn't until she enlisted in the Human Guardian Army with Tiese and headed for the Eastern Gate that she learned of the infinite Wall at the End of the World surrounding the Dark Territory.

In other words, the world as Ronie knew it always had an end. And whenever she surpassed that boundary, there was another one beyond it. Despite this cycle of revelation, she always believed that one of them truly *would be* the complete and utter end of what existed.

"So...you're saying...beyond the Wall at the End of the World, there'll be more land, like the human and dark realms...with meadows and forests and deserts, continuing forever?" she asked uncertainly.

"Mmm," Kirito hummed. "How do I explain this...? Ah. Come over here."

He stood up and extended a hand toward her. Flustered, she grabbed it; he pulled her upright, then guided her over to one of the narrow windows around the edge of the Cloudtop Garden.

"There. Look at that."

His black-sleeved arm was pointing into the darkening blue of the eastern sky, where a pale-white half circle was rising—Lunaria. Ronie and Tsukigake looked up at the large body that was the source of the little dragon's name, Moon Run. Then Kirito said something that seemed extremely obvious.

"It sure is round, isn't it?"

"Y...yes. It's round," she agreed, wondering what his point was.

"That moon isn't a flat circle in the sky. It's a spherical body. That's why it gets bigger and smaller, as only the parts lit by Solus's rays are visible." He then asked uncertainly, "That's something you learn in school in Centoria...right?"

She smiled awkwardly and nodded. "Of course. At the youth training academy, we are taught that it is the golden jewel that is the throne of Lunaria in the celestial realm..."

"Ah. Well, um...the truth is, I've got a fairly strong hypothesis that this world, including the human realm and the dark realm, is actually part of a sphere, just like that one."

"Wh-what?! A sphere?!" shouted Ronie. Her feet suddenly felt unsteady, and she had to focus on her balance. Tsukigake snorted lightly, as if mocking Kirito's hypothesis.

Over the next five minutes, he taught her about the concept of a spherical world—he called it a planet. It wasn't something she found easy to accept, but there was one thing that she did believe:

The ninety-fifth floor of Central Cathedral, the Morning Star Lookout, was entirely open to the sky at its edges. If you stood at the edge and looked out upon the land, you could indeed see a gentle curve along the horizon.

If the world really was in the shape of a sphere, it would only be natural for the skyline to look that way—perhaps—but she couldn't quite put it all together in her mind. She stared at the moon in the sky.

Suddenly, words she'd never consciously thought escaped her lips.

"If this world is the same type of sphere as the moon…then does that mean the moon has meadows and forests and towns with people living in them, too?"

"Huh…?"

Kirito hadn't been expecting that question, either. The black-haired swordsman blinked theatrically, but his eyes softened quickly after that.

"…Yes, you might be right. Depending on the distance to the moon, it might be not just a small satellite but another planet of an equivalent size…But we'll find that out once we go there," he said, so casually that Ronie didn't find it that surprising at first. If anything, it seemed inevitable to her now that he would say something like that.

So Ronie just smiled, leaned a single cen closer to Kirito, and whispered, "When you do, I will accompany you. As your page."

"I'd better build a nice, big dragoncraft, then."

For some time after that, two humans and one dragon silently gazed upon the half circle floating in the distant sky.

3

After the conclusion of the spontaneous tea party, Ronie returned the dishes and silverware to the kitchen, but all the while, she continued to think about what Kirito had said.

Not about the other side of the Wall at the End of the World, or the world being a sphere, or the trip to the moon. She thought about the first thing that had come up in the conversation: the possibility of another war.

She agreed that the wealth of the human lands would continue to breed discontent among the demi-human races. But in all honesty, she found it difficult to see that actually translating into another armed conflict.

That was because of the Peace Pact of the Five Peoples in the Dark Territory, an agreement that bound all the various races of the dark realm. The law was much more primitive there than in the human lands, but at the very least, it did clearly forbid murder and pillaging.

Of course, for hundreds of years, the only law observed in the Dark Territory had been the Law of Power, so even this much was an earthshaking, revolutionary change for them. As a means of reducing the shock in this transitionary period, they were allowed to duel freely so long as life was not taken in the process.

If it came to war, that kind of self-restraint would go out the window.

And the darklanders were no different from regular humans when it came to the soul seal that prevented criminality. That was how, just a few years after the last war, the human realm peacefully accepted so many visitors from the dark realm…

"…Ronie. Are you listening to me, Ronie?"

Her head rose with a start as someone poked her on the shoulder a few times. She'd been practicing her Incarnation in a corner of the training hall on the fourth floor of the cathedral, and at some point, she had fallen deep into contemplation. Today's exercise was Seated Meditation, and unlike maintaining sacred elements or balancing atop poles, it was very easy to become distracted by worldly thoughts during this practice.

Her partner nearby was going straight past worldly thoughts into worldly chat, however. Just to be certain, Ronie glanced over at the training master—Deusolbert of the Conflagration Bow, today—who was giving sword instruction to the lower knights in the center of the hall, and confirmed that he was occupied before whispering to her best friend:

"Sorry, I was spacing out."

She quickly realized that it didn't make sense for *her* to apologize, but her redheaded partner puffed her cheeks out in indignation and whispered back, "What, you didn't hear any of that? I was saying that I want your advice on something."

"Advice?" Ronie repeated, looking her friend over.

Tiese Schtrinen, the apprentice knight who had been her friend ever since the Swordcraft Academy days, nodded at her seriously. "Yes…See, the thing is…I received a proposal."

"What, to spar?! No, you can't duel!" Ronie hissed back immediately, but Tiese just glared at her with her dark-red eyes and said, "No! Just the opposite…Not a duel…but more of a…a family-type…proposal…"

Ronie couldn't figure out what she was implying for several seconds. She just stared with a blank expression until it clicked in her mind. It took all her Incarnation power to prevent herself from screaming out loud in disbelief. She took a deep breath, held it, then exhaled long and low.

Then she inhaled again and asked, very carefully, "You...you mean...*marriage*...?"

Tiese looked down at the floor before her and nodded almost imperceptibly. Again, Ronie had to stop herself from letting instinct take over and asking who had popped the question. But there was only one possible man who might ask Tiese for her hand in marriage at this point in time. That was the elite Integrity Knight and wielder of the Double-Winged Blades, Renly Synthesis Twenty-Seven.

It had been clear ever since the War of the Underworld that he held affection for Tiese. So it wasn't surprising that he would ask; if anything, it had taken too long.

Ronie envisioned the face of the small knight who always wore that shy smile, and she started to congratulate her friend.

But Tiese shook her head quickly before she could get the words out. "I...I still haven't decided what my answer will be," she whispered.

That was a surprise. "Huh...? But why? You don't dislike him. In fact, I thought you liked Sir Renly, too. You're together so often...," she prompted, but Tiese's face grew even more downcast. It was completely unlike the bright and lively girl to look so pained.

"I do like him. But I know why I like him. And it's because...Sir Renly reminds me a little bit of my mentor."

"...!" Ronie inhaled sharply.

Tiese wasn't talking about Swordsman Delegate Kirito, of course. When they'd been primary trainees at Swordcraft Academy, Ronie had served as Kirito's page, while Tiese had attended to another Elite Disciple. His gentle manner and soft smile had hidden a talent for swordfighting and a willpower just as indomitable as Kirito's. Ronie knew that Tiese had admired him with all of her being.

But he was no longer among the living.

Ronie had believed that her red-haired friend had moved past that sadness. She'd come to assume that Tiese had locked those memories away like treasured jewels in her heart and resumed the walk along her path in life.

The tears dripping from those auburn eyelashes told Ronie that this was not the case.

"Tiese…," Ronie said, biting her lip with hesitation. Then she steeled herself and got to her feet. She turned to Deusolbert, who was currently giving orders in the center of the training hall, and shouted, "Instruction Master! Please allow us to conclude today's training session on account of Apprentice Schtrinen feeling under the weather!"

The stern, short-haired man shot her a look like steel arrows, but he did nod without a word to the contrary. Ronie got Tiese to her feet and helped her bow in thanks so that no one could see her face, then left the hall with her.

She put an arm around Tiese's shoulders and quickly descended the stairs with her toward the Rose Garden out behind the cathedral. They gave a little bow of greeting to the large gardener—according to rumor, he had once been a prison guard—and headed blindly through the mazelike paths until they found a little bench far in the back where no one would find them.

In February, even the earliest-blooming breeds of roses in the garden were only starting to bud. The plants shivered in the chill breeze, just leaves and thorns.

Tiese's wet maple-red eyes looked at the rose plants without truly seeing them. After a while, she mumbled, "I believed that… if I was with Sir Renly, I would finally be able to forget about him…I mean, I wished that I could."

"Tiese…" Ronie put her arm around the girl's back. Tiese leaned over limply and rested her head on Ronie's shoulder.

"But…then I realized that I'm always looking for signs of him in Renly's smiles and words and gestures…And Renly knows that I'm not able to forget about him, either. He said it was fine. And he still chose to ask me to marry him. It made me so happy...so happy...but..."

The tears collected on her long lashes again and fell off. This time it wasn't just one pair of droplets, but a steady stream that came and came, seeping into their simple training garb.

"It made me happy, but I really don't want to forget. Deep in my heart, I know that I want to remain with my memories of him forever. And because I'm aware of that...I just can't..."

She sucked in a trembling sob, pressed her face into Ronie's chest, and shouted, "I want to see him...I want to see Eugeo again!"

Ronie held Tiese tightly as she sobbed. Ronie felt her eyes grow hot as well.

Their experience as trainee pages at Swordcraft Academy had lasted for only a month. But to the girls, that time was fate itself—a miracle that would happen only once in their lives.

Long ago, Ronie had sworn to live by that miracle and never love another person in her life. That was probably why she had hoped that Tiese *would* be able to move on and find that happiness for the both of them—a hope that she now realized had been incredibly selfish of her.

Because unlike Ronie, Tiese would never again see that love of her life. She would never again get to touch his hand or speak with him or even gaze at him from afar.

Ronie didn't have the words that would comfort her best friend as she wept. Instead, she rubbed her back and stroked her hair for as long as the moment lasted.

When Tiese's tears finally abated, the darkness of sunset was encroaching upon the Rose Garden. Her head rested atop Ronie's shoulder, and she was clearly wrung out and exhausted. Together, they watched Solus's slow descent in a dull daze.

"......Sorry. Thanks," Tiese offered at last, her voice a miserable croak.

Ronie shook her head. "It's fine. In fact, *I'm* sorry, Tiese. I...I completely failed to understand how you felt. Here I was, just hoping on my own that you would move on and be happy with Sir Renly..."

"It's fine. There's a part of me that does want to do exactly that," Tiese agreed. She took a deep breath; the strength was coming back to her voice now. "I'm going to ask Sir Renly to wait a little bit longer. Maybe additional time isn't going to make any difference... but I just have a feeling."

"A feeling...?"

"Yes. From the moment I saw Kirito's dragoncraft...I had a feeling that something was about to happen. Something was going to change."

Tiese's words forced Ronie to recall that unforgettable moment. A silver light rising endlessly against the blue-sky background. It had filled her with an elation so sharp it had been painful. There was indeed something about that image that was a portent of revolutionary change.

"......Yes. I feel it, too," she murmured. Tiese nodded.

The two apprentice knights sat on the stone seat for a while longer. Eventually, the five-o'clock bell rang. Tiese got to her feet, glanced at Ronie, and said, to the other girl's surprise, "What about you, Ronie?"

"Uh...what about what?"

Her friend's maple-red eyes blinked, and she even seemed to smile the faintest bit. "Have you told Kirito how you feel? Even a little bit?"

"N...no, of course not!" shouted Ronie. She hunched her shoulders and looked around, then shook her head and hissed, "You know I...I couldn't do that. I'm fine with things the way they are."

"If you feel like you have to hold back on account of me, there's no need to do that," Tiese said, with all seriousness.

"No, honestly, it's fine," Ronie insisted. "After all...he has Lady Asuna. And there's Lady Alice, who's bound to come back to this

world eventually, and General Serlut, and…and even Lady Fanatio, perhaps…"

"Oh, Ronie," Tiese lamented with a sigh. "Kirito isn't married to any one of those people. And he outranks even emperors at this point, so if you wanted to go by Basic Imperial Law, he could have…three wives? Four…?"

"Y-you know he would never do something like that!" Ronie said, shouting again, and stood up quickly to avoid letting Tiese see the redness in her cheeks. "Honestly, I'm fine! Just worry about yourself, Tiese!"

She turned on her heel to face away. Her friend sighed audibly once again, then walked over to her. "Well, I guess Kirito himself would never say it…C'mon, Ronie—let's head back. Shimosaki must be hungry by now."

"Yes, I was going to mention that, too. But," Ronie said, glancing left and right at the hedges, "do you know the way back, Tiese?"

"…I was crying. How would I know which way I was going?"

They shared a look. Deep in the midst of the massive rose maze, the two girls sighed heavily.

That night, Ronie lay in her bed on the twenty-second floor of the cathedral but found it difficult to fall asleep.

You just had to go and bring that up, Tiese, she thought, glaring at the thick stone wall that separated her bedroom from the adjacent one. Then she felt bad, realizing that her friend was likely also having trouble falling asleep.

Tiese, of course, was grappling with her first-ever marriage proposal.

I wonder where in the building he did it. What did he say to her? she imagined, finding her thoughts quickly wandering astray. *What if…what if Kirito were to propose to me? What sort of venue would he choose for the proposal? The Morning Star Lookout on the ninety-fifth floor…? Or maybe the rear yard at Swordcraft Academy, where we shared so many memories…? Actually, he might even use his flying arts to take me to the top of the clouds…*

Ronie took a deep breath and pulled the blanket up over her head to knock those thoughts right out of her mind. She told herself that she shouldn't even *imagine* that possibility. There was only one thing she could hope for: that the peace would persist. She could ask for nothing more. Nothing.

She rolled over onto her stomach, buried her face in her pillow, and allowed the fairy of sleep to approach, close her eyelids, and keep them like that.

4

It took only until the lunch banquet of the next day, February 18th, for Ronie to learn that her one simple, humble wish was already in jeopardy.

A lower knight rushed into the room, pale-faced, knelt at Kirito's side, and delivered an urgent report.

A mountain goblin tourist visiting the city had killed a citizen of Centoria.

Both the swordsman delegate and the even-bolder swordswoman subdelegate reacted with a sharp gasp and flared nostrils. Kirito closed his eyes, placed his knife and fork down, and got to his feet.

"Asuna, Fanatio, take command of the Human Guardian Army and city guard. Perform only normal duties and do not allow for any special response to this incident. Where is this goblin now?"

The last question was for the lower knight who'd brought the message. The boyish knight stayed kneeling. "Sir, I'm told he is being held in the South Centoria guard's office!"

"Understood. Thank you for the report!"

And with that, the black cloak swept aside as Kirito began walking, his strides long and brisk. Ronie recovered from her sense of shock and got to her feet, shouting from the opposite side of the large round table, "I-I'll join you, Delegate!"

Kirito paused for a moment to consider this, then nodded. "I'd appreciate it. We'll take a shortcut. Is that all right?"

"H…huh? Um…," she mumbled, catching up to him. Central Cathedral was in the center of the circular city, so once they descended the main stairs and left the south gate, they would be in South Centoria, former capital of the Sothercrois Empire. Major facilities like the city guard's office would be right along the main thoroughfare leading outward, so there weren't any shortcuts, since it was a direct route…

Kirito provided the answer through action. With undeniable purpose, he strode not toward the double doors on the south end of the hall, but to the eastern balcony. Ronie followed after him to the outlook twenty stories in the air—and then had a moment of disbelief.

Just as quickly, Kirito's left arm swept around her back with a brief apology. Before her heart could even skip a beat, there was a strange air-whipping sound, and green light filled her vision.

Ronie started to yelp as she felt herself floating, but the sound caught in her throat as the two of them abruptly shot upward into the air.

They rapidly distanced themselves from the cathedral, and the vast capital grew larger. This sensation was beyond fast. It felt like they were going several times the maximum flight speed of a dragon, yet there was almost no wind resistance—as though he had crafted a film of wind elements that coated her body to eliminate resistance, all the while continuously expending elements behind them to maintain the tremendous acceleration that pushed them along.

By the time she recognized that this was a wind-element flight art—a technique only Kirito could control at this point in time—they were already descending to the ground like a tornado.

There was another strange sound, and the color of the world

went back to normal. Ronie kept her eyes open, fighting off a sudden dizziness, and saw that a huge stone building—by normal standards—was before them. The red sandstone's rough-hewn texture was undeniably that of South Centorian architecture.

Two guards in thick, heavy armor stood at the entrance atop a set of stone steps. They brandished their halberds menacingly, making no effort to hide their alarm over the sudden entrance. Kirito ran straight for them.

""Who goes there?"" demanded the guards, crossing their polearms. From the rear, Ronie summoned up her most authoritative voice and replied, "We are from the Unification Council!"

The guards' eyes swept over to her short cloak's clasp, which bore the crest of the Integrity Knights upon it. Because she was still an apprentice, hers did not have the official number carved into the bottom, but the symbol on its own had the desired effect, fortunately. The guards sprang back to an upright position and smacked the bottom of their halberds on the stone step.

Kirito rushed between them and through the doorway. Ronie followed.

Belatedly, Ronie realized that the swordsman delegate from the Human Unification Council had not brought his sword, his crest, or even his cloak. All he wore was a simple black linen shirt and thick black cotton trousers. The guards could hardly be blamed for not realizing who he was.

But he slipped right between the employees of the guard's office, ignoring their suspicious looks, and headed for the stairs to the basement. Almost as though he knew exactly where to find the goblin in question.

In fact, he almost certainly did. They were about halfway down the stone staircase when Ronie heard the characteristic screech of a goblin's speaking voice.

"...I didn't! I didn't do nothin'! I didn't see nothin'!"

"Don't lie to me, you demi!!" roared a loud human voice.

The second basement level of the city guard's office was a

standard medieval prison filled with stone cells behind gleaming black bars. But upon closer inspection, it was clear that nearly all the cells had dust piled on the floor and hadn't been occupied in years. That was only natural, because the human realm, as a basic rule, did not produce criminals. Only the occasional person who could not remember every last one of the myriad rules and items in the Taboo Index and Basic Imperial Law fell afoul of the law over some trivial matter.

Until now.

At the end of the hallway was a larger room without bars, probably for interrogation. There was a simple wooden table in the center of the dark room, and lying prostrate atop it was a mountain goblin, clearly still very young.

The goblin's small body was being held down from behind by a large, powerful guard. Before him stood a man wearing a captain's uniform with his longsword drawn.

"Let us see if you can continue to tell these foul lies *after* one of your arms has been lopped off!"

Candlelight slid across the face of the flat blade. Ronie was going to shout a command for him to stop, but no sooner had the thought entered her mind than a sharp *ting!* caused the captain's sword to spark. As though struck by an invisible blade, the sword flew from his grasp and hit the far wall.

Kirito had unleashed his secret Integrity Knight technique, an Incarnate Sword. He deflected the captain's attack and plunged into the interrogation room at a full sprint. "That's enough! This entire case is now under the jurisdiction of the Human Unification Council!" he shouted.

"What...?" gasped the captain, stunned at the loss of his sword. When he turned and saw Kirito, his face flushed and the lip beneath his neatly trimmed mustache quivered. He looked ready to yell something when he caught sight of the crest on Ronie's shoulder.

Again, his face underwent a dramatic shift, rapidly paling. The captain and his subordinate fell to one knee and bowed deeply—to Ronie more than to Kirito.

Frankly, this sort of thing had been happening to her quite often when she encountered the people of Centoria. But she still found it very strange. Just a year and three months ago, Ronie had been nothing more than a student. She'd enlisted in the Human Guardian Army in the War of the Underworld and, after a whole lot of swinging her sword around in a daze, found herself promoted to the rank of apprentice knight. She didn't feel like she'd grown into the dignity or status of the role yet.

Of course, if *he* would dress a bit more appropriately, maybe this sort of burden wouldn't fall on her shoulders so often, she thought sourly as Kirito took command of the scene. The young man—dressed indistinguishably from any ordinary citizen of the capital—first nodded to the trembling, terrified goblin in what was meant to be a soothing gesture.

"What is your name?" he asked the young goblin. His yellow eyes blinked rapidly in confusion.

"……Oroi," the goblin said in a pitiful voice.

"Oroi? That decorative feather—are you from the Ubori clan on Saw Hill?"

The goblin nodded rapidly, shaking the blue-and-yellow feather that rose from the leather band around his forehead.

"I see. My name is Kirito. I'm a delegate on the Human Unification Council."

That had an instant effect on the two guards with lowered heads. Their backs twitched, and the young goblin named Oroi's eyes bulged.

"Kirito…I know you! You're the white Ium who beat the Ubori in the pester-bug-catching contest!"

What in the world has he been getting up to? Ronie wondered, but she didn't let her exasperation show.

Kirito nodded. "I still have the centurion's medal I received for winning. Listen to me now, Oroi. I am going to hear the stories of what happened, first from these guards, then from you. No punishments will be given based on what you say, so rest easy and simply tell me exactly what happened."

*   *   *

The guard captain stood on Kirito's command and gave his report with fear and a slight amount of indignant pride.

"At eleven thirty in the morning today, the guard station in District Four of South Centoria received a citizen's report that a demi-human with a bladed weapon was being violent at an inn on Carue Street. Upon rushing to the scene, we found a goblin in the second-floor hallway of the inn with a bloodied dagger. A human man was collapsed and bleeding in the room behind him. The man was the inn's cleaner. He'd been stabbed right in the heart, and his life had been entirely extinguished already. Based on the circumstances, we judged that the goblin had killed the man with the dagger. Thus, we took him to the office building and began our interrogation."

Then Kirito took a statement from Oroi the mountain goblin:

"I came to visit Centoria three days ago in a group of five younglings from the same clan. The others went out into the city after breakfast, but I was feeling sick and stayed behind in the inn to sleep. Someone knocked on the door before noon, so I opened it and found no person, but a dagger on the floor of the hallway. I picked it up and noticed that there was blood on it. I was surprised, and that's when soldiers came up the stairs, yelled some nonsense at me, and arrested me."

"...I didn't do nothin'...I didn't even see anythin'," Oroi finished.

The captain had had enough, however. "I just told you not to lie!" he bellowed. "That dagger does not come from human lands! Only demi-humans would use such a crude cast-iron artifact!"

"N-no! It looks like it, but it's not the same! Goblin swords have the clan symbol on the hilt! No symbol on that sword! It's fake!" Oroi screeched back. That sent the captain into a sputtering rage.

But Kirito held out a hand to silence them both and said, "This is something a quick examination should prove. Captain, where is the dagger now?"

"...It's being kept in the armory on the first floor, sir."

"Would you show it to me?"

The captain gave his subordinate a commanding look. The young guard shot out of the room but returned nearly five minutes later, his face pale.

"......It's not there," he reported.

"What? What do you mean?!" the captain howled.

The guard hunched his neck as far down into his shoulders as he could and repeated, "It's...not there. The dagger isn't in the armory."

Two hours later, Kirito had returned to Central Cathedral—by carriage this time—to deliver an explanation to the principal members of the council. Ronie was allowed to sit at the round table by special exception, because she had accompanied him to the guard office.

The first person to break the silence in the spacious meeting room on the fiftieth floor was Swordswoman Subdelegate Asuna.

"...And where is Oroi the mountain goblin now?"

"We brought him here from the city guard's office. He's in one of the empty rooms on the fourth floor now. I have the door guarded, so technically it's a kind of house arrest," Kirito said, his brow furrowed.

Asuna didn't look too happy, either. "I suppose that's unavoidable until we get to the bottom of this..."

From the opposite side of the round table came Deusolbert's steady baritone. "I take it that the two of you are certain that this goblin did not actually commit a murder?"

"Yes, that's my belief," Kirito admitted. He steepled his fingers atop the table. "Tourism from the Dark Territory to the human realm is handled as a form of cultural exchange between the two realms by this council. When passing through the Eastern Gate, all visitors are required to understand the list of forbidden actions. It's just a simple list of rules, but it forbids stealing, assault, and murder, in the name of the Dark Territory's supreme commander. In other words, Oroi is bound by the dark lands' Law of Power. If he actually had broken that law and killed the inn's housekeeper..."

"His right eye would have burst," finished Commander Fanatio. The rest of the table reflected on those words in silence.

All people who lived in the Underworld, human or demihuman, were created with a piece of sacred arts called Code 871. It ensured that a piercing pain jolted the right eye of anyone in danger of breaking any laws or customs. Actually going through with an illegal action would cause the eyeball itself to explode.

Furthermore, ordinary people never even thought about violating the law. Ronie herself had seen the injustice of the Taboo Index and Basic Imperial Law several times before, but she'd never attempted to break them herself. As far as anyone knew, in the three-hundred-year history of the Underworld, only three people had ever held such desires, acted on them, and experienced the loss of the eyeball—four, if you counted one who tore out that eyeball first.

And there was nothing wrong with the eyes of Oroi the mountain goblin. Ronie had seen that for herself.

"But...," said the hesitant voice of Integrity Knight Renly. The young knight was still waiting for Tiese's answer to his proposal, and Ronie couldn't help but see an extra note of melancholy in his features, whether it was really there or not.

"Murder is the greatest of taboos for all people, not just those like Oroi. We Integrity Knights are granted immunity from nearly all laws, but even we cannot take the life of an innocent civilian. In other words...if someone other than Oroi was responsible for killing that housekeeper..."

"They'd have broken their eye seal," Kirito finished, a bitter grimace on his face. "It's ironic. If we had the old automated senate, we could have that culprit searched out by now."

Asuna shook her head. "No. You can't rely on an inhuman system like that one."

The automated senate, a predecessor of the Human Unification Council, had been a system of remote observation through human power, operated by the Axiom Church. Dozens of powerful casters had had their lives and consciousnesses frozen, rendering them unthinking tools that observed lawbreakers remotely through sacred arts. After the war, the magic binding the senators had unwound, but their minds never returned, and within a few days, all of them had passed away in their sleep.

Kirito exhaled deeply, remembering the accursed sight of them. "Yeah, I know, I know. But...I just can't wipe away this strange feeling I'm getting."

"Which is?" Fanatio prompted, turning her dark eyes on him.

"How do I say this...? The three people who broke the seals in their right eyes didn't do so for the sake of murder. Each case was an act of overwhelming willpower, of resistance against something unfair and unjust. Which would mean, to the killer, that the victim was some kind of symbol of absolute evil who had to be killed by any means necessary..."

Kirito glanced at the papers on the table and continued, "But this housekeeper who was killed, Yazen. As far as I could glean, he seems unlikely to have attracted any hatred from anyone. He grew wheat on the private lands of one of the noble houses for years, and after he was released last year, he started working at the inn. From what we were told, he treated visitors from the Dark Territory as kindly as he did anyone else. If anything, Oroi says that he felt quite friendly toward Yazen."

"Meaning that Yazen couldn't have been in a situation to wield unfair, abusive power over anyone else?" Asuna asked.

"It's basically unthinkable," Kirito replied. "And there is the matter of the missing weapon..."

As soon as he'd heard that the dagger supposedly used to kill Yazen had vanished from the armory, Kirito had questioned every last guard in the office, in the name of the council. But not a single one of them came forward to say they had taken it. The city guard was under the jurisdiction of the Human Guardian Army, which was itself under the jurisdiction of the Unification Council; none of the guards could possibly disobey the order.

So after the dagger in question had been taken from the inn to the armory, either some external person had stolen it, or it had ceased to exist all on its own.

"Does anyone have any opinions on this?" Kirito asked the table.

Deusolbert spoke up immediately. "It sounds as though the weapon was a crude cast-iron dagger. It is possible that a single use was enough to consume all its life, causing it to crumble to nothing in the armory?"

"No…regardless of the quality, a metal weapon would not be obliterated right away. I feel like the metal scraps would still remain in place for a while…"

"Ah…indeed," intoned the large man, crossing his arms with a thoughtful hum.

Suddenly, a thought floated into Ronie's head. She looked around the table to make sure no one was about to speak and hesitantly raised her hand.

"What is it, Ronie?"

"W-well…Um, when Instructor Deu…er, Sir Deusolbert runs out of arrows in his quiver, he replenishes them with sacred arts, yes?" she asked.

The archer nodded. "That's right. Although their priority level is quite inferior to proper steel arrows."

"Well, in the same way…is it possible that the dagger was actually a temporary weapon…made of steel elements…?"

Her idea left the council hall silent for several heavy moments. The stalemate was broken not by Kirito's voice but by his actions. He reached his right hand toward the table and narrowed his eyes.

Three silver lights appeared below his palm. He had produced three steel elements without even a starter, much less the full sacred arts command. The dots blended into one and shone as they changed shape. A sharp point appeared, followed by a curve, while the opposite edge was long and narrow.

The object fell to the table with a *clunk*. It was the goblins' favored single-edged dagger, which Ronie had seen many times before. The thick blade and roughly carved handle seemed very convincing—but there were a few differences that allowed one to discern it from the real thing.

For one, the surface of the weapon was too smooth. And the handle was usually wrapped in dyed leather, but here the entire thing was metal. It would be clear to anyone looking at it that this was a substitute created from steel elements.

Kirito picked up the dagger he'd created and said, "I'm pretty familiar with goblin daggers, and even I can't do any better than this. But the actual murder weapon was finely crafted enough that Oroi himself didn't notice at first...which would mean that a very advanced caster spent a lot of time generating it."

A light metallic ringing overlapped the end of his statement as Kirito rapped the dagger with a light Incarnation blow. That was enough to extinguish the temporary weapon's life, and it shattered like glass, disintegrating into little motes of light that vanished shortly after. Soon there was nothing left.

"...If that is the case, this is a most alarming problem," Commander Fanatio stated, her wavy hair cascading to the side as she tilted her head in thought. "All the advanced sacred arts users in Centoria are either with the army...or otherwise under this council. Which would mean either we've got a traitor in our midst...or..."

Or it's a dark mage from the Dark Territory, everyone else filled in on their own.

If a dark mage had snuck into Centoria and killed an innocent civilian for some nefarious purpose, that would be a situation many times worse than if Oroi the goblin had simply killed Yazen in a fit of rage. Between the tourism and the trade, the two realms' relations were just beginning to thaw; throwing a wrench into the works now could bring about another war.

"Unless...that was the whole idea...?" Kirito muttered to himself. Then he shook his head. "All of this is still inside the realm of speculation. As we investigate further, we need to minimize any effect this incident might have on the populace. We can't stop rumors from spreading, but we *must* prevent secondary or tertiary incidents from occurring as a result of this…How about the army, Asuna?"

She nodded and reported, "I asked Liena…er, General Serlut, to forgo any additional peacekeeping measures aside from the usual. She accepted and agreed…but the former noble faction seems to desire a more hard-line stance: to apprehend all travelers from the Dark Territory. I've sent a written command from the Unification Council, so that should keep them under control for now…"

She paused and took a breath. Asuna's hazelnut eyes shone brightly as she continued, "But if the same kind of incident occurs again, that command is going to lead to overwhelming unrest and distrust toward the council. And if I were secretly pulling strings, causing this incident to happen, I would surely have another one planned."

"Yeah, that's what I would do, too." Kirito sighed. He clapped his hands together to wrap up the topic. "So as a council, we will respond in the following four ways. One, we will publicly announce that a culprit has not yet been identified. Two, we will provide Yazen's family with a full and proper explanation of the situation. Three, we will mobilize maximum manpower to investigate. Four…we will discuss this with the leaders of the dark realm as soon as possible. Does anyone have anything to add?"

Fanatio's hand shot into the air. With some hesitation, she pointed out, "When you say 'soon'…the next scheduled meeting with the dark side is nearly a month away. Are you going to accelerate the schedule?"

"No," said Kirito, shaking his head. "I'm going over to Obsidia to meet with Iskahn myself."

When the meeting adjourned, Solus was already sinking toward the western horizon.

Ronie rushed for the dragon stables on the west side of the cathedral. When she got there, she waved to Tiese, who was looking after Tsukigake for her.

"Sorry; it ran late!"

The pale-yellow juvenile dragon lifted its head from the grass at the sound of her voice, trilled, and came rushing over. She hugged the fluffy body and scratched under its chin, then spoke again to her friend.

"Thank you, Tiese. I'll pay you back…eventually…with favors…"

"You're starting to sound more and more like Kirito," the girl chided with a shake of her red head. "So…how was the meeting?" she asked seriously.

They sat down side by side on a bench along the wall of the stable, and Ronie went over the contents of the emergency meeting. Tiese listened until the end, looking grave. At last she mumbled, "That sounds…pretty bad…"

"Yeah…At the very least, the knights seem to think that it's not possible a regular human from here could have killed the victim…"

"Even though there are those who can bend the laws and find the loopholes that benefit themselves…"

As a matter of fact, the Rebellion of the Four Empires had come about when the remaining emperors had issued edicts declaring the newly formed Human Unification Council to be a traitorous force to the old Axiom Church. The binding force of the law—even once it had been twisted—had been so strong that pacifying the uprising of the empires' imperial guards had required striking down the emperors of Norlangarth, Wesdarath, Eastavarieth, and Sothercrois in order to nullify the edicts. Ronie and Tiese had invaded the Imperial Palace in North Centoria and ended up crossing swords directly with Emperor Cruiga Norlangarth VI. They had experienced his bloated, vicious ego in person.

Both girls rubbed their upper arms simultaneously without realizing it. Tiese then changed the subject and said, "Well, if that's the case, I'll look after Tsukigake a bit longer, I suppose."

"Huh? Why?" Ronie asked, looking puzzled.

Her friend grinned at her and said, "I mean, you're going, aren't you? To Obsidia. With Kirito."

5

There were over three thousand kilors of distance in total between the human capital of Centoria and the dark capital of Obsidia. That was a three-day trip for a dragon. A month by horse-drawn carriage—and at least twice that on foot. In the War of the Underworld, the dark general and emperor, Vecta, was able to move his army of fifty thousand from Obsidia to the Eastern Gate in just five days through secret elixirs and arts. But future examination showed a horrifying side effect: that the maximum life value of any human, demi-human, or animal who'd taken the medicine was steadily but continuously decreasing. The humans had used horses and wagons to travel and hadn't been given the medicines, but the demi-humans, who'd had to march, were still losing life today. The sacred arts masters in the cathedral were busy trying to find an antidote.

When Swordsman Delegate Kirito decided on a sudden visit to Obsidia to address the emergency at hand of the civilian slaying, Ronie assumed he was going to travel by dragon, of course. The wind elements he'd used to fly from Central Cathedral to the guard's office in South Centoria used ample sacred resources, which would be in short supply in the barren Dark Territory. He wouldn't be able to use them with any reliability for the long time it would take to reach Obsidia.

But Kirito did not have his own dragon to fly, so he would need to fly with someone like Deusolbert or Renly. Two riders meant that much more fatigue for a dragon, so she thought it would be presumptuous of herself to ask to go along—until Tiese tried to light a fire under her.

Ronie went from the dragon stables to the thirtieth floor of the cathedral, where Kirito's private quarters were, in order to him prepare for the journey. Asuna met her there with a look of concern and resignation and told her that Kirito had gone to the arsenal.

So she ran another long distance, sharing the subdelegate's concern, back around the rear of the cathedral—the place where the prison had once been—then down a wide sloped path to a large door that was currently open.

Beyond the doorway was a large space of at least thirty mels. Along each of the side walls, five or six young blacksmiths and craftsmen were clinking and clanking away with hammers. In the center of the space, lit by a myriad of light-element lamps, was an enormous man-made object.

It looked much like Unit One, the metallic dragon that had exploded the other day. Beside the dragoncraft, Kirito and Arsenal Master Sadore were vigorously trading opinions—in the form of a shouting match.

"How many times do I have to tell you, boy?! It's still being fine-tuned! It's not ready for full-power flight yet, and you know it!"

"It'll be fine, sir. I'll be flying it horizontally this time, not vertically. As long as we switch out the primary wings for catching the wind, it'll absolutely work!"

"What do you mean, *it'll work*?! I've heard what you're doing—you're going to the capital of the dark realm! We haven't even done a successful test flight, and you think you're going to fly it on a six-thousand-kilor round trip?!"

"No sweat! The heat-element canisters on this one are twice as sturdy, and you poured your blood, sweat, and tears into this craft, Master. This thing could fly ten thousand kilors without a problem. Isn't that right?"

"W-well, I certainly didn't outfit it to fall to pieces right away... but that's not the point! I'm not going to let you talk me into this again, because whenever I do, I suffer more than if a greater swampfly bit me on the bum!"

Ronie felt the blood draining from her face as they argued. Kirito was planning to travel to Obsidia not by dragon or carriage but by using Dragoncraft Unit Two. The incident from the other day replayed itself in her mind. She shook her head and rushed over to them.

"N-no, Kirito, you can't! Arsenal Master Sadore is right! What if there's an accident?!"

"Hey, Ronie. Keep your distance, or you'll get oil on your clothes," Kirito warned, pulling her by the sleeve until she was fifty cens farther away from the dragoncraft. He started off smiling but soon turned serious. "Look, if something happens, I'll fly on my own. All the knights are busy, so I can't ask them to take me to Obsidia, and it'll take a month by horse...I get the feeling that the situation's tighter than we realize. I want to tell the Dark Territory about this situation as quickly as possible, before it's too late..."

"......But there's other danger involved, Kirito," Ronie stated, stepping closer to plead her case. "Whoever killed Yazen and pinned the crime on Oroi the goblin isn't bound by the laws of the Taboo Index. So they could be trying to get you while you're away from Centoria and vulnerable...In fact, this whole crime could have been a trap to make you head to Obsidia!"

"Ah...I see. That is possible...," Kirito murmured. He paused for a few moments, thinking hard.

Sadore broke the silence with a heavy sigh. "Well...it feels like my dream's come true, with the ability to trade techniques and knowledge with the smiths of the dark lands. I wouldn't want things to go back to the way they were before."

"Really...? A master like you still has things to learn?" Kirito asked. Sadore squeezed his gray beard and made a sour face.

"Hmph! Of course. When the guardian army brought back

swords and armor from dark knights, you'd better believe they were remarkable. For one thing, the type of steel they use is completely different from what I know…I can't kick the bucket without learning about the ore and methods they use."

He smacked the shining silver exterior of the dragoncraft with large hands covered in scars. "Kiri, my boy, stop when the heat-element pressurometer hits eighty percent. Oh, and you'd better settle on a unit of pressure measurement already."

"Hey, good thinking! For pressure—let's see…How about one kilom of weight per square cen of area…"

"N-now wait a moment!" Ronie said, interrupting the two men. "The dragoncraft's safety is one thing, but that doesn't change the risk that someone might be after you! As your page, I cannot recommend that you go to the Dark Territory…alone…"

But as she looked up at the head of the dragoncraft during her speech, Ronie noticed something and trailed off. The metal chair—a cockpit, he'd called it—behind the panes of glass looked much longer than that of Unit One. In fact, on closer examination, it looked like there was another seat attached to the back of the cockpit.

"……Um, Kirito?"

"…Wh-what?"

"Does Unit Two seat two?"

"Y…yeah. Unit One blew up because it couldn't supply the frost elements fast enough, but we kind of knew that was likely to happen…This one is designed so that two people can generate frost elements instead, but as I told him earlier, one person should have enough cooling power to fly parallel to the ground, so…"

He spoke faster and faster as he went on, sensing what she was about to say—and then she cleared her throat to cut him off.

"All right, then. In order to neutralize the threat of assassination, you will require the presence of a bodyguard."

"B-bodyguard?"

"But as you mentioned yourself, the elite knights are busy with their own duties, so as an apprentice knight, I shall have to fulfill this mission myself!"

"Wh-what?"

"And I can help monitor the status of the heat-element canisters!"

"Whaaaat?!"

Kirito lurched backward, but before he could argue, Ronie put her right fist to her chest and her left hand to her sword hilt in a formal knight's salute, announcing her acceptance of the mission he hadn't actually given her.

While Kirito was struggling to process what had just happened, Sadore belly-laughed.

"You've lost this round, Kiri, my boy. But I have to say, this young lady's really grown a spine, hasn't she?"

Ronie had succeeded in earning Kirito's permission to accompany him through sheer momentum alone, but that was actually the easy part.

This would be her first time visiting Obsidia, capital of the Dark Territory, and she was Kirito's only travel companion—both firsts for her. She had no idea how one prepared for such a thing, so she returned to her room on the twenty-second floor and pulled out all her clothes and small items so that she could decide on what to bring, when—

A knock came at her door.

"Coming!" shouted Ronie, thinking that it was probably Tiese as she rushed to answer. "Thank goodness, I was just about to ask you to help me pack…"

But when she opened the door, she didn't see her red-haired partner, but rather, a beautiful swordswoman with chestnut-brown hair and pearly-white knight's clothes.

"Ah…! Lady Asuna!" she stammered, starting to do a formal salute, when Asuna reached out to stop her with a smile.

"I'm sorry to intrude when you're busy, Ronie. I was hoping you could come with me..."

"Y...yes, anywhere!" Ronie said. She stepped out into the hallway and followed Asuna.

If this had been the North Centoria Imperial Swordcraft Academy, and it had been an upperclassman calling on her like this, she could easily have imagined being led out behind the school building into a group of students who would say something like *Aren't you getting a little too full of yourself lately?* But this was Central Cathedral, so of course that was not going to happen.

But Ronie could not deny that she felt some amount of guilt and awkwardness around Asuna. Not because she was the swordswoman subdelegate to the Human Unification Council or because she was a real-worlder who'd come to their realm from beyond. It was for a very personal reason that she could not reveal to anyone...

It was one year and three months ago that Asuna had arrived in the Underworld, in the midst of the War of the Underworld.

Ronie and Tiese were in the human army's decoy force at the time, being chased by Emperor Vecta's Dark Army with such ferocity that they might have actually perished before they could have fulfilled their decoy mission. Ronie fought against a dark knight who had slipped into the rear of their formation, but she was very quickly disarmed, and she expected death in that moment—when Asuna arrived.

As she descended from the sky, shining pure and bright against the pitch-blackness of the night sky, Ronie saw nothing but the Goddess of Creation, Stacia, as depicted in the art she'd grown up around in the Arabel family home and on the academy walls. Asuna lifted a scintillating rainbow rapier, created a gigantic hole in the ground, and sent the dark knight trying to kill Ronie tumbling into its gaping maw. In the presence of such godly power, Ronie believed with all her heart that Asuna was Stacia.

Later it was revealed to her that Asuna was, like Kirito—and a dark knight Ronie had fought, and Emperor Vecta himself—a real-worlder, but despite the year since the war, Ronie's gratitude and reverence for Asuna had not dimmed in the slightest.

And yet, when the two came face-to-face like this, Ronie felt an unpleasant twinge in her chest.

That was because Asuna was Kirito's significant other, as everyone now recognized. She had come to the Underworld in the first place in order to save Kirito from the state of mental absentia that had afflicted him.

In the way that they chatted about nothing in particular in the sunlight from the window, the way they passed the salt at the table, even the way that she scolded the swordsman delegate for his reckless behavior, Ronie could sense the deep love that connected the two.

She had never thought about getting in between them. One day...probably not long from now, they would have a wedding, and Ronie was ready to wish them well with all her heart.

But.........but. No matter how much time passed, the throbbing pain deep in her chest did not subside. And she felt like it never would...

As they walked down the hallway and descended the stairs, Ronie was lost deep in thought, so she nearly collided with Asuna when the other girl stopped ahead of her. Accident averted, Ronie looked up and noticed that they were in front of the armory on the third floor of the building.

It was said that, at one time, all but the prime senator, the knight commander, and the pontifex herself were forbidden from opening the armory's double doors, which were carved with images of Solus and Terraria. Now anyone could enter as long as they signed their name in the logbook next to the doorway—but you still weren't allowed to take anything out.

The book, which was full of newly developed hemp paper made of snow-white hemp fibers, rather than the more traditional sheepskin parchment, came with a copper pen that could be refilled with ink, another new invention. Asuna wrote her name down and pushed her way through the doors into the chamber.

It was evening, and no scholars were present, so the two were greeted only by darkness and silence.

Asuna put her hands on the glass tube right next to the entrance and intoned, "System Call, Generate Luminous Element."

Ten light elements appeared within the tube. Then she lifted just one finger and made a wind element this time. The pressure it created pushed the ten elements through the length of the tube, which stretched along the wall, allowing their light to reach the entirety of the armory.

Like the hemp paper and copper pen, this light-element tube was something that Kirito and Asuna had developed; the lamps in the arsenal worked the same way. Unlike with torches and oil lamps, there was no risk of fire, and the light was bright and stable. But even locked inside the glass tube, the light elements reacted to the glass's presence bit by bit until they vanished, requiring someone to regularly refill them by generating more sacred elements. They could replace all the lights in Central Cathedral this way, given that it was full of people with mastery of sacred arts, but it wasn't possible for this kind of item to make its way out into the Centorian market yet.

The light of ten elements caused the armory to shine in glorious fashion. It wasn't Ronie's first time inside, but she was left breathless all the same.

The room was the size of the great training hall at the academy, with sets of armor in all colors arranged along the floor, and a proliferation of swords, spears, and axes in all sizes hung upon the walls up to the tall ceiling. A few of those weapons were Divine Objects of the sort that were awarded to senior Integrity Knights, but Ronie was still an apprentice, and she couldn't tell the difference.

"...It really is a breathtaking sight." Ronie sighed.

"It is," Asuna agreed, "and quite a lot of them have already been distributed to Liena's—er, General Serlut's—army. Kirito wants to sell the majority of them and use the funds to assist the remote towns of the realm and the Dark Territory, but Deusolbert and the others have been quite vocal in their opposition to that."

"Y-yeah, it's very tricky…," Ronie said, the sort of answer you gave when you didn't know what else to say.

She had seen starving mountain goblin children with her own eyes. She knew the importance of sending aid to their realm. Indeed, Kirito's words whispered to her even now: *At this rate, there is going to be another war.*

If that actually did come to pass…she wanted her family in North Centoria, her fellow pupils, the cathedral's knights and artificers, and of course Tiese to stay safe. The weapons and armor here would be very valuable tools for ensuring their safety in that event.

Asuna patted Ronie on the shoulder and gave her a mischievous grin to break the mood. "Having said that, Apprentice Integrity Knight Ronie Arabel…what is your equipment authority level now?"

"Wh-what?! Why would you ask me something like—?"

"Go on—you can tell me."

The second-most-exalted warrior in the human realm was expecting an answer, so she couldn't refuse. But in fact, Ronie realized that she hadn't checked in a while, herself. What if it had gone down? She drew the symbol in the air with her left hand, then tapped her right wrist.

The gently shining Stacia Window that appeared displayed that person's core identity—Kirito called it personal information—so custom dictated that you never look at another's, outside of emergencies. Asuna stepped away politely, and Ronie read off the number next to the label written in sacred language: OBJECT CONTROL AUTHORITY.

"Um…it's thirty-nine."

"Wow! That's almost as much as the numbered knights already," Asuna exclaimed with a grin. "In that case," she murmured, heading for the wall in the back. She inspected the wide array of one-handed swords, picked out four, and brought them back two to a hand. She laid them down on a nearby work table.

"All of these are of priority thirty-eight or thirty-nine. Pick whichever one you want," she said. Ronie was shocked.

A sword with a priority level of thirty-nine was at least at the level of a famous named blade—and possibly even that of a divine weapon. All four of the weapons on the table had finely crafted details and burnished blades that shone like mirrors of different colors. Commander Fanatio's Four Whirling Blades were still using standard-issue swords, however—a mere apprentice like her couldn't possibly take a weapon as fine as these.

"N-no, Lady Asuna...I can't!" Ronie protested, waving her hands and shaking her head.

Asuna giggled. "That's the same kind of gesture Kirito would make."

"Uh...i-it is...?"

"Tee-hee! Don't be shy, Ronie. I already have Commander Fanatio's permission, and remember, you're a hero who saw the war all the way to the end."

"......I'm...not...," she stammered, looking down at the floor. "All I did...was receive the protection of you and Sir Renly and all the men-at-arms—and the soldiers from the real world who came to help...I was completely helpless, even when that black knight was doing such awful things to Kirito."

"That's not true. It just isn't."

Asuna glided over to her and gently put her arms around Ronie. The girl stiffened up in shock, but the sweet, soothing scent of jasmine and Asuna's warmth eventually calmed her nerves.

"It was you and Tiese and Alice who made sure Kirito was protected at all times. To me, you three are the real heroes...I can never thank you enough..."

To her surprise, Ronie found that tears were coming to her eyes. She mumbled, "What is...Lady Alice doing...now...?"

After a pause, Asuna said crisply, "She's alive and well in the real world. After all, she's the hope that connects our two worlds. I'm sure...I'm sure we'll see her again..."

Her arms briefly squeezed tighter, then released Ronie. Asuna smiled for her. "Come—choose your sword. It's not just your weapon, remember; you're going to use it to protect Kirito."

At that point, there was no refusing it.

Ronie stared at the swords Asuna had chosen. All of them were one-handed longswords, but the handle and blade of each were on the slender side. It was clear that she had chosen them not just for the priority number but for how they fit Ronie's build.

From what Kirito had discovered recently, through lots of painstaking experimentation, any piece of combat equipment with a priority level over thirty had not just the life value listed in its Stacia Window but also a power that he called its hidden bonus. When equipped, it might confer an elemental attack of some kind or offer resistance to poison, fatigue, or curses. Some of them made it easier to generate elements of a certain type, increased life regeneration under special circumstances, or conferred greater visibility in the dark or even odd effects like making dogs more friendly.

On top of that, divine weapons that the late Administrator had given to her Integrity Knights were revealed to have enhanced elemental bonuses and other hidden parameters that strengthened sacred arts to match the particular strengths of each knight. In other words, she'd known more about both the weapons and the knights than could be seen with a Stacia Window alone. Central Cathedral's top minds were working hard to produce a sacred art that identified those hidden metrics, but Kirito suspected that it would be a long and difficult process.

The four swords Ronie could choose from must have hidden abilities of their own, but it was impossible to tell by the look of them. She might be able to sense the difference if she tried generating all the elements one by one while holding each sword in turn or running laps around the building to test her life-recovery speed, but there was no time for all of that when she was leaving early in the morning tomorrow.

She stood there, racked by indecision, with no idea of what to use as a basis for her choice, when a faint voice played back from memory.

...This sword used to be so heavy to me, I could barely even pick it up, much less swing it.

The words had been spoken by Eugeo the Elite Disciple when Tiese had been his page at the academy, as he worked on polishing and caring for the beautiful white longsword tinged with the faintest hint of blue. Kirito had grinned at his side, polishing his own black sword, as cups full of steaming cofil tea and exquisitely scented honey pies sat on the table nearby. It was a fond memory from nearly two years ago.

At the time, Tiese and Ronie had been brand-new primary trainees at the North Centoria Imperial Swordcraft Academy. Their high scores on the entrance test made them prime candidates when it came time to choose trainee pages, an honor that went to only twelve out of each class of 120. But the priority-level-fifteen platinum-oak wooden swords were difficult to handle, so they had asked the older students they were serving how to use heavy swords.

Despite its delicate appearance, the Blue Rose Sword was far heavier than a two-handed steel greatsword, Eugeo had said. He lifted it easily and continued, "According to theory, if a swordsman's equipment authority level is higher than the priority of the weapon, it will no longer be too heavy to use. But I don't think that the relationship between a sword and its wielder comes down to simple numbers. Let's say you use a weapon with a much lower priority level than your authority, but you treat it poorly and take care of it less often than you should. When it matters most, that weapon isn't going to do what its owner wants. The reason I couldn't use this sword in the past isn't because I lacked the authority—it's because I lacked the affection for it that I ought to have had...I think."

""Affection...for the sword,"" Ronie and Tiese repeated, mulling over the unfamiliar phrase.

They were both from sixth-ranked noble families, the lowest rank, but their parents spared no expense in getting them good sword training, dreaming of the possibility that they might one day be promoted to fourth-ranked nobles, which would mean they wouldn't be subject to the abusive judicial authority of higher ranks. If they trained so hard that their wooden swords broke, their parents would gladly pay for replacements, rather than scold them for wasting supplies. To them, swords were tools to make dreams come true—not their own, but their parents'—as well as shackles that confined them to futures they did not necessarily choose. So the idea of showing affection to a sword hadn't made sense at first.

But Eugeo had just smiled at the girls and explained, "It's not just swords. Clothes, shoes, tableware…even individual elements generated by sacred arts. All these things will treat you kindly if you open your heart to them. And so will people, I bet."

Kirito had been listening to the conversation without comment. He paused in his polishing of the Night-Sky Blade—at the time, he still called it the Black One—and smirked a bit.

"That's right. Eugeo and I have opened our hearts to each other, too. I can eat his slice of pie at dinner, and he'll just chuckle and let me get away with it."

"I'm sorry, Kirito, but the moment you eat my pie, our bond is broken forever."

Ronie and Tiese had laughed at that. But what Eugeo had said was starting to make sense already.

From that day on, with the dorm manager's permission, the two girls took their platinum-oak training swords from the training hall to their rooms so they could polish the swords and heal the damage they'd done at practice. It did not take long before they were swinging the wooden swords around as if they were extensions of their own arms.

If only those strict but enjoyable days at the academy could have lasted forever. But just a month and a half later, Eugeo and Kirito had used the Blue Rose Sword and the Night-Sky Blade to attack other Elite Disciples in order to save Tiese and Ronie, and they were taken to the Axiom Church as punishment. They escaped from the underground cells and launched an attack on the Church itself, defeating the almighty Integrity Knights one after the other, culminating in the unthinkable toppling of Administrator, the absolute ruler of humanity. And during that fight, Eugeo had perished.

The memory of Tiese sobbing and wishing she could see Eugeo again nearly brought tears to Ronie's eyes anew. She fought them back and reached out with her right hand.

A swordsman doesn't choose their sword. The sword chooses its master. No matter the sword, as long as I give it affection and open my heart, it will respond in kind.

She felt as if her hand were being drawn toward the third sword from the left—one with a black leather handle the same shade as Kirito's hair, but with a silvery guard and pommel that shone softly. The brand-new grip was a bit rough to the touch, but she could tell that if she cared for it, it would soon feel very comfortable to her.

Ronie inhaled, exhaled, and lifted the sword.

It was heavy. The weight made itself known throughout her entire arm, expressing the sword's sense of being, from her fingers up through her wrist, elbow, and shoulder, and into the core of her body.

But it was not an unpleasant feeling. Much like the platinum-oak training sword and the standard-issue sword that she had fought through two wars with, Ronie could sense that this, too, would soon open itself up to her, once she showed it some love.

She squeezed it around the handle and rested the flat of the blade on her left hand, appreciating its presence, when a voice said gently, "Is that the one, then?"

Ronie turned to Asuna and nodded firmly. The subdelegate put the other three back into their sheaths, returned them to the racks on the wall, and circled around the table to stand on Ronie's left.

"You should give the sword a name, Ronie. Once you've decided, go to the management office and have them record your decision in the knighthood's armory registry."

"I…I will."

She felt confused about this at first—she'd never had a sword that needed a name—but it made sense that naming one's sword was the obligation of the owner. In the past, Administrator had apparently created, destroyed, distributed, and confiscated Divine Objects on a whim. But now all the weapons, armor, and accessories in the entire Central Cathedral were accounted for on paper.

Asuna gave her a smile and glanced at Ronie's left side. "What will you do with that one? If you're returning it to the army, I can send it to the command office with tomorrow's courier."

"Uh…ah, g-good idea…," she mumbled, caught off guard a bit by the question.

The standard-issue sword she always kept at her side was indeed owned by Ronie—on the Stacia Window, her name appeared near the sacred letter *P*, for *Possessor*—but according to the Human Guardian Army's rules, it was only on loan. If she replaced her weapon and did not need the old one anymore, it had to be returned to the army.

The leather hilt and sheath were a simple dark brown, and there were no decorations or frills of any sort. It was a practical weapon but was of good make, with a priority level of twenty-five, made of southern croisteel. That wasn't cheap to produce, and Ronie took good care of it, so there was plenty of life left in it.

And truth be told, she should have been given a standard knight's sword a year ago, when she'd been made an apprentice Integrity Knight, but because things had been so hectic at the time, it had been put off. Ronie and Tiese were so attached to their swords that they'd just kept using them.

But now that the swordswoman subdelegate was providing her with a new sword, the moment to move on had arrived. Still…

"……"

Ronie stood there, new sword in one hand, old sword's pommel under the other, frozen in place. Asuna nodded in understanding.

"It's only natural to feel that way. I made things very difficult for Kirito because I didn't want to give up my very first sword."

"Huh...?" Ronie said, startled. She stared. "You didn't, either, Lady Asuna...? Was that...in the real world?"

"Well, not exactly. A long time ago, Kirito and I did battle in a place that was neither the real world nor the Underworld. In fact...I knew nothing about the place, and Kirito showed me how to fight."

"To think that someone with your godlike powers was once a novice..."

"Well, of course I was! I'm just a regular human being like you, Ronie...just a regular girl," Asuna announced with a chuckle. And yet her features were so beautiful, they were beyond human, and Ronie had to squint at their brilliance.

"Um...what happened to that first sword of yours, Lady Asuna?"

Asuna looked down at the palm of her hand, as though reminiscing about the feel of that very blade. Her head rose again. "On Kirito's recommendation, we melted it into ingots—bars of metal—and used those as the material for a new sword. He said, that way, the soul of the sword would be carried on...He can be very sentimental when it comes to swords, you know."

"Hee-hee...That sounds like him."

The girls chuckled together for a few moments. When the moment passed, Asuna said, "But I suppose that doesn't help you right now...We can't melt down a sword belonging to the army, and you already have a new sword..."

"...Actually, after what you said, I've made up my mind. I'll return this sword to the main forces."

She set the new sword down on the table and undid the fasteners on her sword belt. She took the standard-issue sword off, sheath and all, and handed it to Asuna.

"Are you sure...? If I ask Liena, I'm sure she'll arrange for you to keep this one, too..."

"Yes, I'm sure. I've been thinking that this sword is too light for me lately anyway…I'm sure the next person will need it more than me."

"All right," said Asuna. "Then I'll return this to army command with the courier tomorrow."

She deftly took the sword and hung it from the right side of her own belt. An ordinary army sword might be light, but combined with the divine Radiant Light on her left hip, that was a lot of weight. Yet Asuna continued around the work table, as light as a feather, and picked up a black leather sheath with fine silver inlay that she handed over to Ronie.

Ronie took it and bowed her head, stuck the new sword inside, and clasped it onto her belt. She straightened up, feeling the new sense of weight around her body. Asuna stared her straight in the eyes and said, "Ronie…take good care of Kirito."

"Oh…y-yes, my lady!" she replied, a bit taken aback, but she managed to perform a knight's salute. "Apprentice Integrity Knight Ronie Arabel will put her life on the line to protect the swordsman delegate!"

Asuna returned the salute and beamed at her. "Well, don't waste your life out there. I want you both coming back alive, but if Kirito tells you to run, I want you to listen to him."

Ronie sensed a flicker of emotion behind those words. She lowered her hands and asked, "Um…are you sure *you* don't want to accompany him…?"

"Just a bit," Asuna teased, but Ronie was sure that it was an honest answer. The subdelegate just shook her head, though, and continued, "Kirito and I can't both be away from Centoria at this time. There are so many decisions for the council to rule upon, and the former nobles' discontent with us isn't going to disappear anytime soon…"

"I'm so sorry…," Ronie said on reflex. Asuna blinked with surprise, then recovered with a smile and shook her head.

"No, Ronie. It's nothing you need to apologize for. Not at all."

"But…I'm of noble birth, too, and until I became Kirito's page,

I had never held any doubt or misgivings about the system of nobility..."

"Still, your father and Tiese's father worked important jobs for the city garrison and government, didn't they? You weren't like the higher nobles who forced serfs into hard labor on your private estates so that you could live in the lap of luxury."

"......"

Ronie silently bowed again, this time in apology.

On top of a hill not far from Central Cathedral sat the old Imperial Palace, where the imperial government and imperial guard barracks still functioned as before and her father continued to work as a platoon captain.

But the Imperial Knights, who ranked above the imperial guard, had been completely dismantled, and much of the functions of the guard had been transferred to the Human Guardian Army under General Sortiliena Serlut's leadership. In the future, the garrisons belonging to the four empires would be melded into the guardian army so that the military itself could be shrunk to a minimal size. That was because the threat from the Dark Territory had passed, of course—but Ronie did not know whether her father would still have the same job when it came to that.

She knew that if her hardworking father did get reassigned with the unit or transferred to a managerial position, he would continue to perform his duties. He wasn't like the higher nobles who'd lost their massive unearned incomes and had to take first-time jobs that they despised and neglected...she thought.

But within him, and perhaps within Ronie as well, there still had to be that understanding, the self-concept *I am a noble, not a commoner*. And as long as that inherited sense of class consciousness existed, Ronie and the other Arabels were fundamentally no different from the upper nobles.

"Lady Asuna, maybe...," she started to say. But she couldn't follow through.

She couldn't suggest, *Maybe we should eliminate not just the ranks of nobility, but the concept of nobility itself.* Not when she was in a position to become an Integrity Knight, the most exalted class of all, thanks to her privileged head start. And she couldn't separate herself from that ambition. Receiving an Integrity Knight's number, silver armor, a dragon to fly, and the chance to serve Kirito for the rest of her life...It was the one dream Ronie had. It was what drove her.

Asuna inclined her head, urging her to continue. Ronie shook her head and murmured, "I was just going to say...would it be possible to allow Tiese to choose her own sword, too...? She's also been using an army sword this whole time..."

"That was my intention. I've received permission to grant Tiese a sword as well."

"I'm glad to hear that. Thank you."

Hopefully it would help Tiese start fresh and begin a new chapter...Though Ronie knew that it wasn't up to herself to decide that.

They left the armory as the light elements began to fade out and the seven o'clock bells rang. Asuna wrote down the exit time in the book and headed down the great stairs for the general affairs office on the second floor. Left alone again, Ronie gazed at the night sky, with its last tinge of purple, through the huge windows next to the armory entrance. She let out the breath she'd been holding.

At Swordcraft Academy, where she'd spent only half a year, there was a rule that dinner should be eaten by seven o'clock, and if you were late without a valid excuse, you did not receive any. There was no such rule at Central Cathedral, of course, so you could get a hot meal at the mess hall on the tenth floor any time before nine. After that, the kitchen next door had smaller pre-made dishes that could be eaten whenever.

She should have been hungry after all the running around she'd done over the course of the day, but for some reason, she wasn't in the mood to eat, so Ronie went back to her room instead.

Usually she would ride the automatic platform up to the

twenty-second floor, but with the weight of the new sword at her side, she chose to take the stairs and let herself get used to it.

Nearly two years ago, after Kirito and Eugeo had escaped from prison, they'd supposedly raced up these stairs to the fiftieth floor, fighting Integrity Knights along the way. There was no trace of that battle now, but she tried to adopt their mindset as she rushed up the flights until she reached the twenty-second floor, breathing heavily.

Her room was a few doors down, on the right side of the hallway. Because they were apprentices, she shared quarters with Tiese, but her partner was not inside. Assuming she was getting dinner, Ronie crossed through the living room to her own bedroom.

Coincidentally, the layout—a living room with two individual bedrooms—was exactly the same as Kirito and Eugeo's suite in the Elite Disciples' dormitory, though the bedrooms here were much larger. Her space back home before she'd moved to the academy had been only half this size, so Ronie felt quite uncomfortable having so much space. But as she acquired furniture to her liking and changed the design around, she was finding that it felt more and more like home to her.

On the right wall as she passed into the room was a large window facing toward East Centoria. The bed and dresser were on the left, with a small table on the right. On the wall across from the window was a pair of mounting hooks like those in the armory. She walked over, removed her new sword, and placed it there. The black leather sheath fit right in with the interior of primarily dark-brown furniture.

"I'll think it over and give you a name that suits you," she assured the sword, then removed her gray armor and placed it on the stand to the right of the sword mount. Now that she felt much lighter, she wanted to just flop onto her bed. But tomorrow's journey needed preparations, and she had to pack.

Kirito had said she had to keep her belongings within one midsize standard-issue suitcase, which meant she had some hard decisions to make. As a girl turning seventeen this year, she wanted to bring as many clothes as possible, but this wasn't just a journey for travel's sake; she was going as Kirito's bodyguard, so medical items and sacred arts reagents took priority.

Ronie would need to examine what she had on hand so that she'd know what she should stock up on at the apothecary. But first...

"......I want a bath...," she mumbled, leaving the room and bringing just a change of underwear.

The residential quarters of the cathedral spanned from the twentieth to thirtieth floors, with a shared bath for each floor. Normally, Ronie and Tiese used the one on their floor, but every now and then...especially knowing she was about to leave the cathedral for an extended time, there was a different place she liked to go.

Ronie continued all the way down the hallway to the vertical shaft at the northernmost point of the floor. She set the metered knob to its highest point, the ninetieth floor, then pressed the metal button. That released the necessary number of wind elements to fill the canister at the bottom of the levitating disc and soon sent Ronie upward.

Half a minute later, the platform's ascent began to slow until it came to a stop, and she opened the metal door again.

There was another short hallway ahead that ended in a split to either side. White curtains hung from the ceiling just before the split, and mysteriously enough, the curtains were painted with a very stylized form of the character for *bath*.

The hanging curtains had been Kirito's idea, and he'd painted the character on them, but no one knew exactly what the purpose of it was. Only Swordswoman Subdelegate Asuna seemed to recognize it, and she kept her silence with nothing more than a stifled, slightly annoyed smirk.

Each time you walked down the hallway, you approached the curtain in bemusement, lifted it up and out of the way—the bottom had a long vertical slit in the middle—then arrived at the split. After that, there were more hanging curtains for the left and right paths.

The dark-blue curtain on the right side said MEN in white. The rouge-red curtain on the left said WOMEN. These displays at least made a certain kind of sense, aside from why they needed to be written on hanging curtains. So Ronie headed through the curtain marked for women. The hallway turned to the right toward a spacious room.

The room, which featured large shelves running across it like partitioning walls, was not empty. Three women from the artificers' department were dressed in the one-piece outfits of the eastern style, drying their wet hair as they sat in wicker chairs along the wall. They started to stand when they saw Ronie, but she held out her hands to keep them in place.

The women paused, half-risen, then sat back down and bowed their heads in greeting.

"Good evening, Lady Knight." "How are you, my lady?"

"Good evening," Ronie replied politely, then scurried away to the far side of the room. Once she was behind the shelves, she heaved a sigh of relief. She hadn't been raised to the level of apprentice knight all that recently, but she still found it very strange to receive deferential treatment from older women. Even if she became a full-fledged knight, Ronie felt certain that the bold, proud manner that Commander Fanatio wore would never come naturally to her.

She quickly took off her clothes and placed them in a basket on the shelf, along with the change of fresh underwear she'd brought, then grabbed a white towel and pressed it to her front as she opened the glass door in the back.

She was met with a sudden onrush of thick white steam, so she quickly stepped in and shut the door behind her. The steam dissipated, and she was greeted by a sight that never failed to take her breath away.

The huge space took up about half of the ninetieth floor of Central Cathedral. The floor and pillars were made of pure-white marble, and the south and east walls were one huge pane of glass, creating a full night view of Centoria. This alone made it even more luxurious than the old imperial throne room, but even more stunning was the incredible amount of heated water that covered the floor, which sank down in a series of steps.

The bathing chamber was 40 mels from north to south and 25 from east to west. The walkways that surrounded the bath were 2 mels wide, and it was about a mel deep, giving a rough calculation of 874 cubic mels. Converted into liquid measurement, that was an astronomical 874,000 lirs. And in fact, on the other side of the western wall—the side beyond the men's curtain—was a symmetrically arranged bath of the same size, so the total amount of water was twice that volume.

This was the Great Bath, or as Kirito liked to say, "The most luxurious facility in Central Cathedral."

Before the War of the Underworld, only thirty Integrity Knights had been allowed to use this space, and there had been no dividing wall, so it had often been the case that only a single person had twice as much water to themselves. But with the restructuring of the institution, the bath was opened up to all the other faculty members and split into men's and women's sides.

There were about twenty people using it now, but since the bath was the size of a small lake, there was no sense of crowding at all. Regardless, Ronie walked to the empty southeast corner and dipped her toe into the crystal-clear water. It felt hot at first, but her skin adjusted as she stepped down the rows until she sat on the final step.

With hot water up to her neck, she felt an overwhelming sense of release that simply didn't exist in the practical-sized baths on the residential floors. It numbed her head and caused her to moan, "*Unhhhh...*"

"Great big baths are just the best."

"They really are...," she agreed, then looked around in a panic. Somehow there was someone sitting just to her left.

When the steam trailing over the surface broke apart and revealed the face of the person right there, Ronie backed away again.

She had light-brown hair short enough that the wet ends of it stuck to the nape of her neck, and large light-blue eyes. She was sitting one step higher than Ronie and was as small and delicate as a child. In fact, she looked like a girl of about ten years old, but on the inside, she was nowhere near as innocent.

"G-good evening, Lady Fizel," she said, just as awkwardly as the women in the changing room had greeted Ronie. The girl flicked the surface of the water with her fingers.

"Don't give me that 'Lady' stuff. You're older than me, Ronie."

"B-but…you are a proper knight, Lady Fizel…"

"*Grrr.* Why do I feel like we've done this bit a hundred times already?" griped the girl, who lifted her legs level with the surface and kicked her feet to splash. Her name was Fizel Synthesis Twenty-Nine.

During the War of the Underworld, she'd had a special "numbered apprentice" status, but afterward, she'd been given a proper promotion, and she was now a full-fledged Integrity Knight. She had silver armor fitted for her small stature and a dragon named Himawari, or Sunflower, which she used mostly for reconnaissance, all over the human realm.

"I haven't seen you lately, Lady Fizel. Were you out on another mission?" Ronie asked.

Fizel sank down until her mouth was at water level. "Yep. The remnants of the western Imperial Knights are acting strangely, so I went to check on them. In fact, Linel is still over there—I just came back to report in and restock on supplies."

"I see…Aldares Wesdarath V was the only emperor whose body was never found—isn't that correct? Do you suppose there's a relation there?"

"Mmm, Sister Fanatio's Memory Release art completely burned the western Imperial Palace to the ground, you see. The emperor was already an old man at that point, so I can't imagine he survived. But there are certainly people who would like to make you think he's alive."

She might have been blowing bubbles into the surface of the

water as she talked, but it certainly wasn't the sort of thing a ten-year-old child talked about. Fizel, however, was not necessarily as old as she looked. She was born in the cathedral and, along with her partner, Linel Synthesis Twenty-Eight, had not undergone the Synthesis Ritual, but for some reason, when Administrator chose to make the girls apprentice Integrity Knights, she'd performed the art of life-freezing on them as children, rather than at the peak of their growth and life value, as was customary. In other words, the girls would maintain their current appearance without aging—visually, at least.

The thought made Ronie want to hug the girls tight to comfort them, but she had never actually done so. Not only were they senior knights to her, but it was said that they'd had official numbers as apprentices because they had killed the previous knights with those numbers. Furthermore, they had reportedly tried to kill Kirito and Eugeo with knives coated with paralytic poison, and during the war, they had also slaughtered the entire invading goblin troop that had swung around to the rear of the Human Guardian Army, by themselves. In other words, the stories were innumerable, and all were horrifying. There was nothing frightening about talking to them, per se, but they were clearly people you wanted to make sure you were showing proper respect.

"More to the point, Ronie—"

Ronie snapped to attention awkwardly with the shock of hearing her name.

"Y-yes?"

"I heard the news." Fizel grinned, floating on the surface of the bath. "You're accompanying Kirito on his trip to Obsidia?"

"Er, well, I..."

Their trip to the Dark Territory was top secret, but Ronie soon realized that it was probably pointless to keep secrets from the cathedral's best intelligence agent.

"...Yes, I am," she admitted.

"If you could get me a souvenir, I'd appreciate a selection of arcane herbs from the dark mages guild."

"...I...I'll try..."

"Ah-ha-ha-ha! I'm just joking," Fizel said, flashing an age-appropriate grin. She sat upright on the higher step and gazed at the scenery through the glass window.

Ronie followed her lead and saw, at the bottom of the darkness, the lights of East Centoria flickering like stars. Many of its buildings were built in the traditional wooden style, and rather than oil lamps, they used lanterns made of paper or thin fabric. They made the light from the city feel a bit warmer, somehow.

Far beyond, seven hundred and fifty kilors away, was the Eastern Gate. Obsidia lay over two thousand kilors beyond that. She'd learned from the academy that the city's name came from the sacred word *obsidian*, but the teacher hadn't known what it was supposed to mean.

She found herself asking rather silly questions like *Will I understand when I see it for myself? Am I really going over there, to the other end of the world?*

"When you go there...," Fizel murmured. Ronie looked back at the youthful senior knight.

"Yes...?"

"Hmm...Well, the war's over now, so hopefully I'm just overthinking this..."

There was no one nearby, and the forceful flow of steaming water from the spout on the wall would have drowned out any sound that might have gotten through, but Fizel leaned closed to Ronie in a conspiratorial whisper anyway.

"Keep your eyes open in Obsidia. Always watch yourself."

"I...I will..."

"The Peace Pact of the Five Peoples is active now, but the dark lands are still ruled by the Law of Power," Fizel warned. "Commander Iskahn is the most powerful man at present, and he's in the faction for peace; Lady Sheyta is there, too, to help him keep things under control on the surface...But even here, there are loopholes and gaps in the many layers of the Taboo Index and Basic Human Law that bind us, which unscrupulous people can interpret to their own benefit. Over there, the law is much more vague, so there could be even more wicked folks lurking everywhere you go."

Ronie felt as though the temperature of the water dropped. She shivered involuntarily, and Fizel reached out to pat her on the hand. "Sorry, sorry, didn't mean to scare you."

"N-no, I'm fine. I will take your advice to heart."

"Mm-hmm. By the time you come back, our missions will probably be over, so we can invite Tiese along for a little wrap-up party to celebrate."

"Yes, that would be wonderful!" Ronie agreed.

Fizel grinned and stood up. "In that case, I'm getting out now," she said with a wave. As the young knight's feet slapped against the marble surface of the walkway, Ronie bowed to her one more time.

Fizel was the twenty-ninth knight. The thirtieth was Alice, the Osmanthus Knight, but she had left for the real world at the end of the War of the Underworld. The thirty-first, Frostscale Whip Eldrie, had perished protecting Alice. Their numbers were now retired, so if Ronie and Tiese were promoted to official knights, one would probably be Thirty-Two, and the other, Thirty-Three.

She longed for that day, without a shadow of a doubt. But it also filled her with a painful apprehension, a sure sign that she wasn't ready for it yet. Ronie's skill with the sword and arts, along with her mental strength, was still nowhere near that of the upper knights like Renly, or even Fizel and Linel, the child ones.

One step at a time.

Slow or not, the only way to move forward was one step at a time. As long as she did not give up on her self-improvement and tried earnestly to learn, she would reach the place she wanted to be.

"……Ronie Synthesis Thirty-Three……"

She looked around quickly to make sure no one was there. Nobody had heard her sample the name, but she let her head sink under the water out of sheer embarrassment. She blew bubbles in a steady stream until she ran out of breath at last.

6

Dawn rose on February 19th.

At the enormous dragon stables along the western wall of the cathedral grounds, Ronie rubbed the neck of her little dragon, Tsukigake.

The juvenile creature trilled lightly and narrowed its eyes in pleasure—or perhaps residual sleepiness. The dragon wasn't the only one; Tiese's red head nodded as she leaned against the silver fence. Ronie had wanted to get to bed early last night but couldn't sleep, so she and Tiese had spent much of the night talking in the living room.

Though they'd been together nearly two years, one had to wonder how they had never run out of topics to get completely engrossed in. That was probably just how it worked with best friends. It had taken Kirito and Eugeo years to leave Rulid in the distant north, travel to Centoria, enter the academy, and advance to Elite Disciple status, but they'd always enjoyed chatting, debating fight tactics, or simply occupying the same space in blissful silence.

Tiese was at a major turning point in her life. If she accepted Renly's proposal—or even if she didn't—Ronie hoped they could always be best friends.

"...Well, Tsukigake, I have to go. Do what Tiese tells you and be a good dragon."

Ronie straightened up, and the little dragon lifted its head to chirp, "*Kyuru!*"

When Tiese finally woke up again, they went to the arsenal behind the cathedral, where Dragoncraft Unit Two had already been pulled out onto the stone surface outside.

It wasn't standing upright the way Unit One had been; instead, it rested with three legs on the ground, like it had inside the hangar. In fact, the feet of the craft weren't clawed like a dragon's feet; they ended in wheels.

Kirito, Asuna, Fanatio, and Arsenal Master Sadore were standing near the head, along with one other woman, who looked about the same age as Ronie. That woman was wearing an arsenal work uniform, performing sacred arts on the craft. Ronie realized that this was the generation of wind elements for it to fly. She leaned over to her partner, who was carrying her suitcase for her.

"Hey, Tiese, do you think that's...?"

"Oh yeah. That's her. She was the operator of the levitating platform before it got automated."

"Ohhh...She's really pretty."

"I agree, but from what I hear, she's been alive at least as long as Deusolbert."

"W-wow, I didn't know..."

Kirito noticed that the two of them were talking a short distance away, and he waved a hand. "Hey, Ronie, Tiese, over here."

"Ah...coming! Good morning!" "Morning!" They called in tandem, approaching.

The sky was still dark overhead, but now that it was outdoors, Unit Two was even bigger than Ronie had imagined. Not only were there two pilot seats, but the wings were as long as a real dragon's, and the exhausted apertures in the back were huge. The whole thing was about 40 percent bigger than Unit One, a good seven mels long.

Now that she was looking at it, she suddenly felt nervous about riding it, but accompanying Kirito had been her idea in the first place, so there was no use getting cold feet. She forced herself to stop thinking about the fiery end of Unit One and greeted Kirito and Asuna with a bow.

"I'm sorry. I know I'm a little late."

"No, it's still ten minutes to five."

It had been quite a while since the four-thirty bell, but Kirito's announcement about the time was quite confident. He glanced at the new sword on her left hip and smiled.

"Thanks for agreeing to watch my back, Ronie."

"I…I will!" she stammered. She was going to say *with my life*, but the memory of what Asuna had said last night stopped her. Instead, she squeaked, "I'll d-do my best!"

It was a bit childish, but it earned her warm smiles from both Kirito and Asuna. Once she had greeted Fanatio and Sadore as well, she was ready to grab her luggage from Tiese. The case was heavy, being so packed full of supplies. But where was she going to put it on the dragoncraft…?

"Kirito, I've finished loading the wind elements," said a voice from behind them. Ronie and Tiese spun around to see the former operator of the levitating platform. They were struck by her delicate beauty; she seemed more suited to a church frock or some noblewoman's dress than the sturdy work outfit of the arsenal.

"Thank you, Airy. I appreciate it," said Kirito. The girl named Airy bowed without any change in expression, then stepped back to stand next to Sadore.

Just then, the gentle chimes of the five o'clock bells played from the cathedral. Kirito promptly clapped his hands.

"Well then, I suppose we should get going! I'll take that case, Ronie," he said, holding out his hands. She gave it to him, and he opened a small door on the side of the dragoncraft and stuffed it into a space that seemed designed for cargo. With that done, Ronie turned to give Tiese a big hug. They didn't need to share

any words; Ronie thought, *I'll be back before you know it*, and Tiese returned the sentiment by thinking, *Just come home safely.*

Ronie loosened her grip, looked into Tiese's eyes one last time, and headed toward the front end of the dragoncraft, where Kirito was waiting for her. He ushered her to the ladder going from the ground up to the craft's head. She timidly climbed up until she reached the little elliptical room with seats located front and back.

The back of the front seat was tilted downward, so Ronie took off her sword and worked herself into the rear seat. It was simple leather stretched over a metal frame, but the material was valuable, supple greater-red-horn leather, so it felt more comfortable than she'd expected.

Kirito ascended the ladder soon after, returned the seat to its proper position, and took his place in it. Sadore pulled the ladder away, and Kirito turned a handle that lowered the glass ceiling over the tiny space with a clank.

All of a sudden, Ronie's heart was pounding. She swallowed hard.

Tsukigake was still too young to fly, but she had ridden tandem several times on Renly's Kazenui, Fizel's Himawari, and Linel's Hinageshi. The first time or two it had been scary, but soon the delight of carving through the wind outweighed her fear. She didn't think she had any particular fear of flying, but now that she was in an artificial dragon largely made of metal and was riding *inside* rather than on its back, she felt more baffled than excited. For one thing, there were no wings meant for beating the air, so how would they return to the ground once they'd lifted off?

The sight of Unit One exploding flashed through her mind again, causing her to shiver. "Ah...um, Kirito?"

"What is it?" he asked casually from the front seat.

Ronie leaned forward, closer to his head, and asked, "Does this dragon fly by unleashing heat elements like the last one?"

"That's right."

"If we start flying and making an incredible roar early in the morning, won't it startle everyone in the capital awake...?"

"I suppose it will," Kirito murmured, then explained, "but the problem is, we don't have a long enough runway here, so we can't take off horizontally. Unfortunately, we'll have to cheat a bit for Unit Two's takeoff and landing."

She didn't really understand all the words he'd just said. "Ch-cheat...? Meaning...?"

Kirito just grinned at her without answering. He grabbed two metal rods attached to the front part of his seat. His hands started glowing faintly, and she held her breath.

What happened next was not the work of elements. Kirito's willpower itself was glowing as it interfaced with the laws of the world. That was the light of Incarnation.

The steel dragon shuddered like a living thing. A moment later, it felt like the body was being lifted upward.

Ronie looked through the glass lid in alarm. Gradually, the sight of gray cobblestones and Tiese and Asuna waving wildly grew more distant. Kirito was lifting this enormous dragoncraft solely through willpower and imagination.

It did seem like cheating, Ronie thought as she waved back. As their ascending speed picked up, the people on the ground got smaller and smaller, until they were hidden by the white of the morning mist. The Rose Garden to the north of the arsenal and the white walls of the cathedral came into view instead.

She lowered her hand and looked forward to see nothing but dark-blue sky before sunrise. The beauty of the faint-red glow on the horizon took her breath away.

Once they reached the height of the Great Bath on the ninetieth floor of the cathedral, the dragoncraft stopped climbing and began to proceed parallel with the ground. This was a smooth acceleration, like gliding across water—nothing like the powerful beating of a real dragon's wings. There was no sound, aside from the low howling of the wind around them. Unless someone happened to be looking up at the early morning sky, no one in Centoria would notice their presence.

With that concern solved, another one gripped her mind.

"Kirito…are you sure you can control something this big with just Incarnation?" she asked, leaning toward the front seat. She was instantly worried that she might be distracting him and breaking his focus, but his voice returned as casually as ever.

"For the time being, yeah. But I feel like it'll be tough to fly it like this all the way out of the human realm…"

"Oh…I see…"

The unfathomable willpower of the swordsman delegate left her stunned.

As an apprentice Integrity Knight, Ronie underwent Incarnation training, but she found it difficult to advance to the next stage, whether with more-practical exercises like Pole Isolation (standing on only one foot atop a narrow pillar) or Element Communing (preserving elements in midair with willpower) or even with simple Seated Meditation, where all she had to do was sit on the ground and concentrate.

For one thing, even expert knights such as Fanatio and Deusolbert considered Incarnate Arms, which moved an object about the size of a short sword, and Incarnate Sword, which slashed with unseen blades, to be their ultimate techniques. So Kirito's Incarnation power was completely off the charts if it kept a huge, metal, two-passenger dragoncraft aloft.

"…And even with your overwhelming Incarnation, you can't cross the Wall at the End of the World…," Ronie murmured.

Kirito grimaced. "It could be that I'm just lacking discipline… but there's no point in crossing if I'm the only one who can do it. We need to make it possible to fly large dragoncraft or levitating platforms like the one in the cathedral at regular intervals so that the people of the Dark Territory—the people of the entire Underworld—can come and go freely."

As Kirito's ideas so often turned out to be, the concept of attaching a levitating platform to walls whose height couldn't even be measured was dumbfounding. Ronie gazed absently through the window.

The dragoncraft had traveled out of East Centoria, so only fields and meadows covered with the recent snow were visible below. It was a chilly sight to gaze upon, but by March, the planting of wheat would begin, and new greenery would cover the land.

Ronie envisioned that sight for a few moments, then asked, "Um, Kirito...do we even need to try crossing the Wall at the End of the World? Why not just move the Dark Territory people here? There's plenty of uncultivated land, with room for more fields and villages..."

Kirito didn't have an immediate answer for her this time. Eventually he murmured, "If only everyone in the human realm thought the way you do, Ronie."

"Huh...? Wh-what do you mean by that...?"

"Well, uh...let's see. At present, we estimate the total population of the realm to be eighty-two thousand. The latest reports suggest that the Dark Territory's is about the same. The human realm is about one million, seven hundred and seventy thousand square kilors, over half of which is undeveloped forests and plains. So as you say, in terms of land area, we could support the doubling of the total population...I think."

Ronie found herself shocked by this for a different reason. "What...? Is it true that the population of the dark realm is over eighty thousand?! And during the war, Emperor Vecta formed an army out of fifty thousand of them...?"

"That's how it adds up...Fanatio told me that every able-bodied person over there gets made into a soldier. It's pretty awful. But I'm sure it's a custom brought about by the barren land of the Dark Territory. In that world, the ones who fight and take for themselves are the ones who survive."

He paused there, leaning back against the seat. The craft briefly wobbled and straightened out again, as though he had momentarily lost focus.

"...Like the dark realm, the human realm has its own shared understanding that's been built up over three centuries of history. They know the people of the Dark Territory as terrifying monsters who come over the End Mountains to steal children and livestock. With the opening of trade, there are more tourists and traders going between the two sides, but longstanding prejudices don't change so quickly. You can control people with new laws and taboos, but you can't eliminate the instinctual fears and desires that drive them…" His voice was grave. Ronie didn't know what to say to him.

He had enough Incarnation power to lift a metal dragon and defeat Administrator and even Emperor Vecta, but Kirito was not a god. He was just a person born in a different world, with the same troubles, worries, and anguish that Ronie dealt with.

Kirito always got back on his feet, no matter how much he was hurt, and he'd saved the Underworld from an existential danger. He'd received no public honors for this and continued to fight for the sake of the world. Ronie wanted to help him achieve the unprecedented feat of peace between the human and dark realms, but all she could think about was the danger of the path ahead, and she had no helpful advice to offer.

She had forced her way along on this trip through sheer momentum and determination, but now she could only wonder what the point of her presence was.

Kirito seemed to sense her sudden change in mood and said, "Listen, Ronie, I'm glad you came along. I'm more likely to accidentally scare the kids over there on first meeting."

"Um…you are?"

"I feel like the stories and rumors precede me now…but I guess I shouldn't be surprised, after the war we had…"

Kirito exhaled to reset his mood and said firmly, "Well, we're safely away from Centoria, so let's switch from Incarnation flight over to elemental flight."

"O-okay!" she chirped. Then she said, "What…should I be doing…?"

"Good question. Maintain a communing state with the elements, like you did during Unit One's test flight, and tell me if anything starts going wrong."

"Roger that!" she replied.

Kirito gave her a strange signal—he pointed his right thumb upward—and then gripped the metal handles again. "System Call, Generate Thermal Element!" he chanted.

His hands glowed red as heat elements appeared inside the metal handles, which were apparently hollow. With Incarnation, he moved them through the tubes down into the canisters in the middle of the dragoncraft.

Even the swordsman delegate found it difficult to control the massive craft and tiny elements with Incarnation at the same time, however, and there was more shaking. Ronie reached forward and put her hands on Kirito's shoulders without thinking.

She didn't add any incantations, but she could sense the flow of sacred power swirling through the air around them easing. The shaking of the dragoncraft subsided, and the ten heat elements stayed firmly in place within the canister.

"Thank you, Ronie," Kirito said, patting her hand and exhaling. "Discharge."

The command released all the heat elements, creating a massive burst of flames. The pressure pushed the flames toward the end of the canister at the rear of the dragoncraft. Along the way, the flames mixed with the wind elements that had been loaded into a different canister before takeoff, and it was compressed into a single burst, like a gout of flaming dragon breath that roared out of the exit aperture at the back of the craft.

The sudden burst of acceleration pushed Ronie back in her chair and trapped the air in her throat. The clouds floating by outside the window shot past them. In terms of speed alone, Kirito's wind-element flight from Central Cathedral to the city guard's building in South Centoria had been faster, but at present, the dragoncraft was under almost no Incarnation control. In other words, an adept sacred arts user, with practice, might be able to fly it just like Kirito was doing now.

Ronie briefly wondered if *this*, more than trying to tackle the Wall at the End of the. World, was the real benefit to humanity, but that inkling of a thought was quickly snuffed out by the roaring that filled the tiny space.

She clutched the frame of her seat with all her strength and shouted, "K…Kirito! How fast is this dragoncraft going right now?!"

"Hmm, let's see," said Kirito without much concern. "The maximum speed of an Integrity Knight's dragon mount is about a hundred and twenty kilors per hour, and it's more like eighty for continuous flight over long distances without fatigue. But I'd bet this thing is going about two hundred and fifty kilors per hour right now…"

"T…twice as fast as a dragon??!"

"I bet we could get to three hundred per hour at maximum output. But Sadore said to keep it at eighty percent," Kirito said, pointing at one of the many rounded dials in front of his seat. The needle attached to it was trembling a few ticks short of the highest speed.

"Three hundred kilors in an hour…," Ronie murmured. She shook her head, unable to fathom such a thing by any practical measurement.

What she could understand was that if the dragoncraft continued on at this speed, it would reach the distant end of the earth—Obsidia Palace, three thousand kilors away—in just half a day. And there was no one who could do anything about a craft flying at such a speed and height.

Was there really a point to me coming along? she wondered again as she allowed herself to sink into the vibration of the seat.

They crossed the End Mountains and continued flying through the red sky of the Dark Territory for about fifteen hours. Despite two breaks along the way, her butt and back were starting to ache when Kirito finally pointed ahead.

"There, you can see it."

She squinted over his shoulder and saw a faint light on the distant, darkened horizon. It was just a vague blur at first, but as they drew closer, it turned into a collection of countless individual lights.

"So that's...the capital of the Dark Territory...," Ronie murmured hoarsely. "You've been there before, haven't you?" she asked Kirito.

"Yes, but just the one time. And it was an unofficial visit, so I hardly got any time to see the castle or the town or anything."

"I'm guessing that will be the case this time, as well," she murmured.

He seemed to take her statement as one of disappointment, because Kirito looked over his shoulder and grinned at her. "Not only is this visit unofficial, I didn't even let Iskahn know ahead of time. See, there are certain things we can get away with this way."

"G-get away with...?"

She felt yet another sense of foreboding—it seemed to happen quite frequently when she hung around with Kirito—and looked out the window again.

The dragoncraft was traveling at less than half its maximum speed, but that was still fast enough that the lights of the town ahead were starting to take clear shape. Unlike the neatly compartmentalized districts of Centoria, the plethora of lights below seemed to have no patterns, except that in total they made a kind of crescent-moon shape. In the middle was a blackened rock mountain that stuck up into the sky like a spear.

The lights continued up the mountain, because the mountain itself was Emperor Vecta's palace. That mammoth formation, shaped by its exposure to the elements over many years, was said to be just as impressive as the Axiom Church's Central Cathedral—but in the darkness, you could make out only its silhouette.

"About ten kilors to go...Okay, let's switch back to Incarnation flight and land this thing," Kirito said, to Ronie's shock.

"What? We're going down this far away?"

"Yep. I'm sure that it would cause a riot if we lowered this craft right onto the city or palace, out of nowhere..."

Kirito squeezed the metal rod that he called a control stick, and he used Incarnation to steadily extinguish the heat elements burning away inside the sealed canister. The roar that filled the tiny room (which he called a cockpit) steadily grew quieter until it was gone.

Without its source of propulsion, the dragoncraft lost altitude until Kirito firmly held it aloft with Incarnation again. Ronie had experienced this landing sequence before, when they stopped for a break, but she still felt nervous, and she squeezed the frame of the seat harder.

She made a mental note to ask for some kind of bar near the rear seat to hold on to, once they got back to Centoria. As they descended, she felt stages of weightlessness similar to the experience of using the levitating platform at the cathedral. With a little thump, the dragoncraft fell still, and Kirito stretched in the front seat.

"We made it, Ronie. Now we fly with our own power."

Despite carrying two swords, a small bag, a large bag, and the unexpected luggage that was an entire additional person, aka Ronie, Kirito crossed the remaining ten kilors with wind-element flight in a blink. According to him, given the weak sacred power of the Dark Territory, ten kilors was about the limit you could achieve there for stable flight.

Inevitably, Ronie had to be pressed tight to Kirito's body during the flight, and while it caused her heart to race at first, that feeling was promptly neutralized by the realization that being in his arms made her nothing more than another piece of luggage to carry around.

They landed on a wide street heading to Obsidia's castle town. The cobblestones were as worn and smooth as if they'd been polished, indicating that humans, demi-humans, and carriages created heavy traffic during the day. But after ten o'clock at night, there wasn't a soul to be seen.

This was usually the time that Ronie would be in bed already, so the moment her feet hit the ground, the fatigue of the long travel and the late hour both hit her at once, and she had to shake her head to maintain focus. This was where her guard duty truly began...

Except that as he attached the Night-Sky Blade to his left hip, Kirito's next words were "Let's go search for an inn."

Ronie blinked. "Uh...w-we aren't going to the castle?"

"The gates will be closed at this hour, and I'm sure Iskahn's already asleep. If we try to sneak inside and any guards spot us, they'll assume we're assassins."

"...Good point..."

They'd crossed the entire Underworld in order to address a murder mystery that involved a mountain goblin being framed for the deed. It would be a bad joke if they got confused for assassins now.

"All right. But what inn will allow humans like us to stay without being suspicious of—," Ronie started to ask, but Kirito was already rummaging in his small leather bag. He pulled out something small; by the faint light of the town ahead, she could see that it was some sort of solution.

"Now, if you'll excuse my reach," Kirito said, handling the solution. She leaned closer to see.

"*Eengk!*" she yelped as he wiped something on her face. She froze with shock at the sensation, and Kirito quickly used both hands to apply the solution. He rubbed her cheeks, her forehead, her ears, and even below her chin, then stepped back to inspect her.

"Yeah, that looks good."

"What...*is* this...?"

She rubbed her cheek herself, but the sensation was already gone, and nothing came off on her fingertip. Kirito just grinned and did the same to his face. His skin was a bit more tan than that of Ronie and Tiese, who'd been born in Norlangarth, but it was still around the average tint for a resident of the human realm. Now it was getting darker and darker before her eyes.

In just a matter of seconds, Kirito had turned a shade of brown that resembled cofil tea. In fact, he looked like he came from Sothercrois...or even the Dark Territory...

And then it hit her.

"Oh...y-you just disguised us as darklanders?"

"Yep. Both you and I have dark hair, and it's winter now, so I figure that if we just change our faces a bit, we might pass."

Belatedly, Ronie realized that her own face had changed, and she touched her cheeks again. Kirito saw her do it and smiled. "It's fine, I swear. You actually look pretty good." Her cheeks grew hot beneath her hands.

"Th-this isn't permanent, right?" she asked, a little sharper than necessary to hide her embarrassment.

He looked a bit nervous. "Y-yeah, of course. Cutoconia the herbalist assured me that it would wear off on its own in about eight hours."

"On its own...? What is it made of?"

"It sounded like we're better off not knowing," Kirito mumbled. He reached out to fix her ruffled hair, then looked to the east.

In Centoria, there was a large gate and a guard station at the border to the city, but Obsidia's castle town seemed to have nothing of the sort. There was just an increase in the density of buildings as the street went on, until you were in the middle of a city. There were no guards in sight.

"...I think we should be fine, but if anyone happens to ask us who we are,...Let's see. We can say we came from Faldera looking for work, and we're hus— We're brother and sister."

Ronie let go of her cheeks and repeated, "Fal...dera? What's that?"

"It's a town about thirty kilors to the southwest."

In truth, she also wanted to know what Kirito had been about to say before he changed it to "brother and sister," but she decided not to pursue that topic. "All right. Let's go, then."

She pulled the hood of her cloak over her head and reached down to the bag resting on the street to grab the still-unnamed sword resting on it and hang it from her belt. She reached down again for the bag this time, but Kirito lifted it first.

"Ah…You know, I can carry my own bag…"

"Oh, but I'm your big brother now, and brothers always carry their sisters' luggage around," he said with a grin. With her bag in hand and his own leather satchel over his shoulder, he took off down the road. She had no choice but to follow, wondering what she should call him once they were in town.

The light grew brighter and brighter as they walked along the road, and they soon began to pass other humans and demi-humans. It made Ronie both relieved and nervous.

On first glance, nearly all the buildings in this castle town seemed to be made of a blackish stone, and there were few instances of trees or water; overall, it felt stifling compared to Centoria. But the lamps that were attached everywhere on houses and roadside posts cast off red, yellow, and purple light, even late at night, giving the place a colorful, festive ambience.

"What are those lamps burning?" she asked.

"Ore they mine from nearby mountains," Kirito answered promptly. "A chunk the size of your fist will burn for ten days, apparently."

"Wow, that sounds very handy."

"You could sell it for a hefty price over in the human realm, I'm sure, but handling the material is tricky. It'll burn all on its own unless it's submerged in water, which makes long-distance transport difficult…"

They walked onward, chatting about this and that, and the area up ahead got steadily busier. Noise was emanating from an open square with a number of carts along the edges and with tables set up in the middle where many men were eating and drinking.

About half of them were dark-skinned humans, with more than a few orcs and goblins as well, but they sat at separate tables. Even after the Peace Pact of the Five Peoples, the differences that separated the races that lived in the Dark Territory had not gone away, Ronie realized.

Kirito saw what she was looking at and said, "It's still a huge change that they'll drink in the same place at all. See how the pugilists and the orcs are sitting at adjacent tables and occasionally trading comments?"

"Oh, you're right…It looks like they're toasting, too…"

A burly pugilist with no shirt on despite the February chill lifted a wooden mug and shouted something, and an orc sitting next to him slammed his own mug into it. As she watched this happen from the edge of the square, Ronie found herself murmuring, "The orcs came to rescue the pugilists during the War of the Underworld when the pugilists were nearly wiped out…I hear the orcs still speak with godlike reverence about the 'Green Swordswoman' who led them."

Ronie hadn't been there herself, but she knew that the Green Swordswoman, Leafa, who'd vanished with the conclusion of the war, was Kirito's sister, who had come from the real world.

Kirito's darkened face pinched with pain very briefly, but he soon regained his usual aloof expression. "Yeah…there's no doubt that our quick peace with the Dark Territory was thanks to Leafa. And that's why we have to protect this peace, now that it's here."

"…I know."

Ronie could keenly sense the fundamental unease she'd been trying to forget all day now lapping at her heels like waves. Kirito patted her on the back.

"Well, it's late now, but we should get some dinner. I'm tired of eating travel rations."

"Huh…? W-we're going to eat *here*?"

"Yeah, doesn't the food from the carts smell so good…? If I were able to resist this kind of temptation, I wouldn't be getting yelled at by Fanatio and Deusolbert all the time," Kirito said, as though that excused his behavior. He fixed his grip on the bags and began to walk into the square.

Ronie had no choice but to follow, and soon a fragrant smell was tickling her nostrils and reminding her of the emptiness of her stomach. Six carts were lined up along the edge of the square, but at a glance, it was hard to tell which of them sold what.

In these situations, Ronie usually waffled between different options until Tiese got fed up and chose for her, but her red-haired partner was not here. She looked over at Kirito, intent on assessing the decision-making ability of the swordsman delegate. He was muttering, "Mmm, those skewers look good...but look at the time—I should probably go with the noodle soup over there...Oh, but those steamed buns, too..."

Chagrined, she recalled that Kirito was usually the one who couldn't make up his mind and needed Eugeo to decide. Then another thought occurred to her, and she tugged on Kirito's cloak.

"Um, Kirito? Before you start buying any food...do we have the money they use over here?"

"......"

His face transformed from shock to despair in several distinct stages.

In the human realm, currency came in four categories: thousand-*shia* gold coins, hundred-*shia* silver coins, ten-*shia* copper coins, and one-*shia* iron coins. Technically, there was also a ten-thousand-*shia* platinum coin, but it was used only for transactions between the government and major merchants, so ordinary citizens and lower nobles never actually saw or used them.

To Ronie, *money* had always meant *shia*, but of course, the coins stamped by the Axiom Church with a profile of Stacia's face were not going to be used in the Dark Territory. They must have their own currency here.

Having just realized this himself, Kirito's shoulders slumped, crestfallen.

"...They don't use money in the cathedral, so I completely forgot..."

"W-wait…Are you saying you didn't bring any *shia*, either…?"

Ronie wasn't sure how to react to this. She just stared at the delegate in numb disbelief.

There was a gold coin sewn into the back of Ronie's sword belt, in case of emergencies, but it wasn't going to be useful here. Then she detected an even bigger problem and asked Kirito, "Does this mean we can't stay at an inn, either…?"

"Well…I suppose it does," he agreed gravely.

Ronie sighed, right in his face. "If we had gone in to stay without a coin to our name, how were you planning to pay for it?"

"I dunno. I just figured it would come out of my inventory automatically—*ka-ching*," he said, a sequence of words that meant nothing to her. He was still looking at the food carts with stubborn dedication, then finally he surveyed the palace that jutted through the night sky.

"Ah well. We'll just have to pray that Iskahn's still awake and sneak into Obsidia Palace…"

Who was just saying that the last thing we want to do is be confused for assassins?!

Ronie took a deep breath, preparing to tear into him, when she saw a large figure appear over their heads as they whispered between themselves in a corner of the square.

"…?!"

She looked up, forcing herself not to reach for her sword as her instincts screamed at her to do so. It was a very large man, probably one mel and ninety cens in height.

His exposed torso, rippling muscles, and studded leather belt, along with the many, many scars running across his bronzed skin, were the marks of a pugilist. Beneath his scraggly hair, his face was so red that even by the light of the ore lamps, it was clear he'd been drinking for quite a while.

"What's wrong, pal? Not enough money to eat?" he said. There was no overt hostility in his voice, which helped Ronie relax the tiniest bit.

Kirito nodded, not bothering to hide the pathetic look on his face, and in the voice of a starving man—she couldn't be sure whether this was an act or not—said, "Y-yes, that's right...I came here from Faldera with my sister, looking for work, but we ran out of funds along the way."

"Ah, from Faldera? My old man's from there!" the man said. Ronie instantly felt a chill run down her back at the thought of having to discuss memories about a place of which she only knew the name and nothing else, but fortunately it did not turn into that. Instead, the man slapped Kirito's shoulder with a massive hand as leathery as a glove and said generously, "Then it's my treat, from one Falderan to another!"

"Th-that's not what I was aski...," Kirito started to protest, seemingly feeling guilty, but the pugilist pushed him onward into the square. Ronie hurried to keep up with them.

The pugilist guided them to the smallest and dingiest of the six carts in the square. The owner, who stirred an ancient pot with a long ladle, sported such long, overgrown bangs that the only thing she could discern about him was the fact that he was a human male. In the corner of the faded cloth banner hanging from the canopy of the cart were the words OBSIDIA SOUP, which seemed to be the name of the dish being served.

"This is the best stuff in this square. Though none of my companions seem to agree!" the drunken pugilist said, laughing uproariously.

Kirito tried to back away, his cheek twitching. "I—I don't know, sir. I'm getting a bad feeling about..."

"That's what they all say at first. Just take my word for it and give it a try. Three bowls, Pop!" the pugilist proclaimed to the server, pulling three copper coins from the small sack hanging off his belt and dropping them on the long, blackened board. If these were the same value as the copper coins in the human realm, then this mysterious Obsidia soup was ten *shia* to a bowl. That would be very cheap, even for cart food.

The server set out three wooden bowls on the board without a word and poured heavy ladlefuls of the pot's contents into them, then provided wooden spoons. He picked up the coins, still silent, and returned to his stirring.

Unperturbed by the sullen nature of the man—either because he was used to it or because he was drunk—the pugilist picked up two of the bowls and presented them to Kirito and Ronie. At this point, they had no choice but to accept, so they thanked him and accepted his gift.

Inside the bowls was something that could be described only as a thick brown soup. It contained many things, but the broth was so muddy that it was impossible to determine what had been stewed into it at a glance.

At the urging of their new friend, who picked up his own bowl, Ronie sat down next to Kirito at an empty table and grabbed her spoon, trying to summon her courage for the task.

She scooped up a small amount of the liquid, which looked like stew that had been slow-cooked for three whole days, blew on it, and took a taste. At first, she found it very spicy, but that soon turned to a sourness, then a strange mixture of richness and bitterness, followed up by a faintly sweet aftertaste.

"……Kirito, what would you call this flavor…?" she asked him under her breath. He finished tasting his own, looking thoughtful, and stared down at the wooden spoon.

"I would say…the flavor's pretty similar to what I remember, but it's strangely edible. In fact, I might even say this is good…"

"What…? You've eaten this before?"

Kirito looked over at her, seemingly coming out of a daze, and shook his head. "Oh, n-no, never mind. There was a place that served a similar dish in…a place I lived long ago. In fact, the guy serving it even looks a little like him, but that doesn't matter…The soup that I'm familiar with was like a fight between spiciness, sourness, bitterness, and sweetness where everybody loses. But this Obsidia soup, it's like the flavor is more comfortable, more mature. It's kind of softened, in a way…"

"That's it! I knew you'd understand, pal!" said the pugilist, who had already finished a third of his bowl. He slapped Kirito on the back. "They say this pot's been bubbling the same mixture, with ingredients and water for the broth being added, ever since Obsidia was founded over two hundred years ago. I bet there ain't a single dish like this over in the human realm! Ga-ha-ha-ha!"

"Y-yeah, I bet not...," Kirito agreed awkwardly.

Ronie struggled to contain her shock. "T-two hundred years...?! How does the food's life last for so long?! Soups and stews usually go bad after five days, even in winter..."

"That's just how great Pop is," the pugilist stated proudly, pounding his own chest as though the cart owner were a prized family member. "Pop never steps away from the cart, and he keeps the flames just low enough so the pot never cools off or burns. If you keep the flames going like that indefinitely, the life of the pot's contents never goes down. That means he eats his own three meals a day out of this very pot...and you can't say that for anyone else in the dark realm—or the entire Underworld itself—if you ask me."

"E-every day...?" Ronie repeated, shocked. She looked at the cart. The sullen owner was staring down and stirring the pot, his face hidden as usual.

"...Does that mean his life was frozen, too, so he's been alive... for over two centuries?" she wondered.

This seemed to be an entirely new concept to the pugilist. He looked from the bowl to the cart several times, back and forth, then shook his head. "Nah. Who do you think he is, that pontifex they speak about from the human realm? I'm sure it's just a family tradition passed down through the generations."

"Y-yes, of course," Ronie agreed. She scooped up a blob of something in the middle of the bowl and timidly inserted it into her mouth. Within one or two bites of what seemed like poultry, a rich flavor flooded her tongue. Despite the very odd flavoring, this soup might prove to be addictive with time—perhaps. Eventually.

Kirito had gotten used to it much faster than Ronie had, and he had already emptied his bowl. He exhaled with great satisfaction. "Ahhh, that was good…I think. It might not be a stretch to say so…"

Then he stretched and bowed deeply to the pugilist sitting across the table. "Thank you very much for this meal, good sir. I will never forget the kindness you've shown us."

"Oh, no problem at all," said the man, who had long since finished his own bowl. His drunken face broke into a sloppy smile. "If you find good work here and are stable enough to eat all the Obsidia soup you want, then you can return the favor with a bowl for me…if all goes well…"

He slapped his face with a meaty hand and rubbed it until the smile was gone. "See…you might find it harder than you think to earn gainful employment for both brother and sister in Obsidia, my friend."

"Oh…really? But it's so busy here in the middle of the night. The city seems bustling to me…"

"To appearances, sure. But that's just because there are more people now…and even that won't last much longer…"

A goblin selling booze walked by, and the now deflated pugilist bought a suspicious-looking little bottle. He took a swig, grimaced, and handed it over. Kirito accepted it with some hesitation, sipped at it, and began coughing violently. The pugilist took the bottle back with a wicked grin.

"This is what the flatland goblins settling near the town make. It tastes like crap, but it's cheap, and they sell a good amount of it. Because of that, the alehouses in the city are losing business, and the merchants guild is fuming. Before the war, the guild would have hired mercenary troops to raid the goblin settlements and put them all to the sword, but now that the Peace Pact of the Five Peoples is around…"

"So you're saying…because of the demi-humans moving to Obsidia, humans are losing their jobs…?"

"It's not just because of them. There are lots more humans, too…Folks like yourselves," the pugilist said with a shrug. He glanced up into the darkness above. "If you came from Faldera, then you don't need me to tell you that the land's too brittle all over. Humans and demi-humans have suffered from hunger and thirst since the start of time. The great war that ended the Age of Blood and Iron started out as a squabble over a single lake, they say…"

Ronie and Kirito didn't know much about the history of the Dark Territory, so they could only nod in silence. The pugilist took another swig of cheap liquor and continued, "And our ancestors managed to survive through this harsh wasteland because of that saying: One day, the gate to the human realm will open, and we'll all live in a fertile land of dreams."

Ronie felt herself stiffen at these words, but the pugilist didn't notice her reaction.

"You and your sister were probably too young to be part of the campaign, but when Emperor Vecta came back a little over a year ago and said we were gonna invade their realm, the excitement was overwhelming, as you might imagine. The saying was finally comin' to pass, we thought…But the Integrity Knights from the human lands were even more monstrous than we realized…and we didn't know there would be an army on the other side, either. It was all chaos and combat; and before we knew it, the emperor had been beaten by some swordsman from afar, and the war was over…"

Ronie glanced sidelong at the "swordsman from afar," whose forehead was beading with sweat, even more than when he had tasted the infamous soup. The pugilist, who couldn't have imagined who he was actually talking to, propped his cheek against his fist.

"If the war had kept going, mighta been the end of all the five peoples. So I got no complaints about peace with the Human Empire, but at the same time…our dream of having fertile lands is gone, too. That's the reason all the goblins, orcs, and young humans have come flooding into Obsidia…They think there might be a slightly better life here. But just because the city's big doesn't mean there are limitless jobs to be done. If you're human, you might get a job in the knighthood…but you and your sister look too scrawny for that kind of work…"

The pugilist's eyes, heavy from fatigue and booze, blinked sleepily at them, and Kirito decided that the time was right. He bowed and said, "Thank you for everything, sir. The Obsidia soup was delicious…I will repay your goodwill one day."

"Yeah…Good luck, kids…"

And with that, he finally fell asleep. They got up, careful not to disturb him.

Elsewhere around the square, the goblins and orcs had left as well, leaving only a few of the pugilists behind, passed out at the tables. Most of the carts were packing up for the night, except for the soup stirrer, who continued his careful work. Apparently, it was true that he slept with his pot.

"…Guess we should look for an inn to stay at," Kirito said, yawning.

"But what about the cost?" Ronie quickly reminded him. "I don't think we're going to get lucky again like with the food."

"Oh, it'll work out." He grinned and started walking to the eastern exit of the square, leaving her with no choice but to hurry after him.

The closer they got to the center of the city, the more ore lamps there were—and the more noise. But after what the pugilist had said, the colored lamps seemed more like meager resistance against the barren land, and the buzz of conversation was just a reflection of accumulating frustration.

Kirito solved the money issue by selling a knife he had tucked away to a roadside merchant, a surprisingly simple solution. He also got directions to a cheap place to stay, and they continued walking. The swordsman delegate was less talkative than usual, so Ronie tried her best to keep the conversation light, without making too much noise.

"So the money here is called *vecs*. Do you suppose one *vec* is roughly equivalent to one *shia*?"

"Huh…? Oh, s-something like that. Still, that would mean that ten *vecs* for a cup of Obsidia soup is really cheap…"

"Are you hoping to have another bowl?"

"I can't hide anything from my former page," he said, looking more like the old Kirito, and patted Ronie on the head. Then he pointed to a building on the right up ahead. "That looks like the place the roadside merchant recommended."

The blackish stone walls featured a cast-iron sign bearing the sacred letters *I-N-N* like inns in the human realm. A vague sense of unease rippled through Ronie's chest, but it dissipated before she could put word to what was bothering her.

"…What's the matter, Ronie?" Kirito asked, but she shook her head.

"It's nothing."

"All right…It's been a long day. Let's get some sleep."

He shifted his grip on their bags, one big and one small, and headed for the door beneath the sign. Despite being nearly midnight, the inn was still open for business, fortunately. The owner was a human woman in her forties, and she gave Kirito and Ronie a very piercing gaze for the better part of a minute—but she did not treat their story about being siblings coming from Faldera for work with any skepticism.

Kirito did not seem to anticipate that this made-up background story might cause new problems. The woman promptly said "If you're siblings, you'll want one room, then!" and started pushing them to a room on the second floor without hearing a single word of protest—and only after she had made sure to collect the hundred-*vec* nightly cost.

"Make sure you're out by the ten o'clock bell in the morning! I've already put out the fire for the bath, so if you want to wash up, you'll need to visit the bathhouse farther ahead. If you say you're a guest with me, they'll give you a discount!"

It was hard to tell if this was an act of kindness or cheapness on her part. But moments later, the woman left them to go back downstairs.

Ronie stood there in mute shock, and Kirito said uncomfortably, "I'm…sorry about this, Ronie. This only happened because I was fixated on staying at an inn…"

"N-no, it's not your fault…"

"I'll just find somewhere outside to sleep. You can use the room."

"F-find somewhere…?"

"There's bound to be some side alley or park where I can rest. I'll be safe on my own. You get a good night's sleep. I'll be back in the morning," Kirito said, and he made to leave out the window, but she grabbed his cloak first.

"N-no, you can't, Kirito! It's too cold. You can't go copying the pugilists, or you'll get sick!"

Inside the room, there was a simple bed, along with a two-seat sofa. Even Ronie was too tall for her legs to fit all the way on it, but it wouldn't be impossible to sleep that way.

"I'll sleep on the sofa. You take the bed. Please."

"H-huh? B-but…doesn't the Taboo Index or Basic Imperial Law have some rule somewhere about unmarried men and women sleeping in the room?"

"No, there's no such rule. What it forbids is k-kissing on the lips…and……"

"And what?" Kirito asked, leaning closer. She grabbed him by the shoulders and pushed him forcefully toward the bed.

"N-no matter what the rules are, you are the human world's swordsman delegate, and I'm already an Integrity Knight, apprentice or not! So it doesn't matter!"

"Aaah!" Kirito yelped at being shoved, tripping on his feet and landing on the bed. She quickly undid the string of his cloak to take it off, yanked the boots off his feet, and shoved him into the bed properly.

She pulled the padded comforter up to his neck, smoothed it over him, and then patted him politely on the chest through it. The delegate looked at her with chagrin and said, "You're like my mom or something, Ronie."

"Oh...s-sorry, it's just that when I was a child, this is what my mother did for us."

"I see...I'd like to meet your parents one day," he murmured, gazing up at the ceiling. Ronie remembered going home the previous month, and the memory threatened to dredge up all the marriage offers her parents had dangled in front of her, before she shooed the thought away.

"I...I'm sure they would be delighted to see you," she said, thinking, *Though my little brother would be happiest of all.* Kirito grinned and closed his eyes. Within a matter of seconds, she could hear him breathing peacefully. He'd seemed fine all throughout the day, but the act of flying that dragoncraft three thousand kilors must have been mentally exhausting.

Relieved that he had gone to sleep in the bed without protest, Ronie took off her own cloak and, with a bit of trouble, put out the ore lamp by pouring water inside it.

She sat down on the sofa against the wall, placed her shoes neatly on the floor, and lay down on her side. As she expected, her toes stuck out, but using the heavy cloak of fine western wool as a blanket, she found the cold did not bother her.

She felt sleep coming on at once but resisted it by staring at Kirito's profile, which was lit by the soft glow of the city through the window. She wondered what would happen if he really did come to visit her family...and then something occurred to her.

Leafa the Green Swordswoman couldn't be Kirito's only family member. Back in the real world, he must have parents, perhaps other siblings, and friends. But Kirito had never spoken about his family.

Does he...ever wish he could go back?

Of course he must. Ronie's family was still in Centoria, very close by, and even she got homesick for her parents and brother sometimes.

But she didn't have the courage to ask Kirito about that. What would she say if he admitted to her that he wanted to go home someday? She didn't even know if there was a way to get back to the real world now.

I wonder what kind of place it is.

The real world was a source of fear and distaste, not fondness, to all the Underworlders who'd fought in the great war. Ronie was no exception. Just the thought of a world producing those terrible red knights who'd wiped out the armies of the human and dark realms made her limbs grow cold.

But on the other hand, the real world was also the home of Kirito, Asuna, and the warriors who'd come to the aid of the Human Guardian Army during the war.

In the Underworld, there were good people and bad people. Perhaps the real world was the same. But that thought wasn't enough for her to wish the gate between them would open again.

What had Alice the Integrity Knight seen and felt when she traveled to that distant place? Would the day come when she might return and speak of those experiences...?

Ronie found herself shaken by the same odd feeling she'd gotten when she saw the sign on the outside of the inn, but the weight of her eyelids was growing irresistible, and she fell asleep for the very first time in a foreign land.

7

The sound of heavy bells tolling woke Ronie up, and she saw bright light already streaming through the thin curtains over the window.

Blinking and rubbing her eyes, she sat up, checking around the room in a haze of sleepiness as she wrapped herself in the cloak she was using for a blanket. Very quickly she spotted the black-haired swordsman fast asleep on the bed nearby. Eight hours had passed, and the effect of the herbs had worn off, because his sleeping face was pale again and surprisingly cherubic. It put a smile on her own face.

But then the facts sank in: She had spent a night in the same room as Kirito, different beds or not. The realization jolted the sleep from her mind, and her face flushed. She pressed her hands to her cheeks, which were cold from being outside of the cloak, and took deep breaths until she calmed down. Promptly after, she bolted to her feet.

Ronie walked over to the bed and gently shook her superior's shoulder, saying, "Wake up. Wake up—it's eight o'clock."

It was at that point that she realized all the time-telling bell melodies she'd been hearing since last night were exactly the same as those played by the bells at Central Cathedral.

What could explain that? Why would the bells attached to the

Axiom Church in the human realm and the bells in this far-flung dark capital play the same tune? The question fell out of her mind when Kirito mumbled and tried to wriggle farther under the blanket.

"*Mmrm…*bit longer……"

"No, don't go back to sleep!" She pulled on the blanket, but Kirito clung hard to the end with both hands, protesting like a stubborn child.

"Five minutes…just three more minutes, Eugeo…"

Ronie gasped. She let go of the blanket and put her hand over her mouth, stepping backward.

Kirito's best friend, Elite Disciple Eugeo, had died nearly two years ago in the fight against Administrator. But to Kirito, his time with Eugeo wasn't yet the past. Like Tiese, he was still living it.

She snuck back to the couch and sat down again.

Swordswoman Subdelegate Asuna slept in the same room as Kirito. She would probably know his secret thoughts, the deep sadness that he kept hidden beneath the surface. And yet she had found a way to stay by his side, always smiling and warm and gentle…

When she got back to Centoria, Ronie would have a proper conversation with Asuna. She couldn't reveal the secret feelings she harbored, but the two of them were united in their desire to help Kirito.

To her surprise, about three minutes later, as promised, Kirito sat up. He looked around the room with eyes that were more than half closed.

When he spotted his companion, he yawned hugely. "Morning, Ronie."

"G…good morning, Kirito."

"Sorry, slept in a bit…What time is it?"

"The eight o'clock bell just rang."

"I see. Then we'll be in time for checkout…er, for the time she wants us out."

He yawned again and got out of bed, then headed for the window and yanked the gray curtains open.

"Hey, Ronie, check it out. You can see the palace," he said.

"Really? You can?"

She got up from the sofa to join him. Sure enough, off in the distance and a little to the right, looming over the chaos of the city, was the clear figure of the pitch-black palace, soaring into the sky.

It tore through the morning mist, which was far redder than what she knew back home. Being carved largely out of natural rock, it was understandably rougher hewn than Central Cathedral, but that gave it a kind of beauty all its own. Even Kirito, who was seeing it for the second time, exhaled long and low with admiration.

"Unlike Central Cathedral, which Administrator built with her superhuman powers, that palace was carved out of the rock by mortal hands," he said.

Ronie marveled at the thought. "How many months—? How many *years* must it have taken…?"

"They say it took over a hundred years…Well anyway, we should be going. If we take too long, it'll be noon before we know it."

"Let's not forget who was responsible for sleeping in!" snapped Ronie. He gave a mischievous little grin to duck responsibility and began to put the bags together.

Once they had reapplied the cofil-tea solution and paid for their night, they found a city lit red by the morning sun rather than ore lamps.

The inn was over five kilors away from Obsidia Palace, but the walk hardly felt long at all due to all the novel sights.

The road got wider as they approached the palace, and the buildings lining it also grew bigger and fancier. But the number of people walking the streets dwindled, and there was no longer a single demi-human in sight.

Eventually, they came to a river of considerable size—at least by local standards—and a large stone bridge spanning it. On the other side was a big gate, behind which was a gentle upward slope that led to the abnormally sharp obsidian spire that was the palace.

Kirito came to a stop at the foot of the bridge. Ronie asked him quietly, "So...have you figured out how we're going to get into the castle?"

The swordsman's face tilted thoughtfully. "Hmm...I don't think that merely acting like darklanders is going to be enough to get us into the palace...And if we try to fly up to the top of it, the guards are going to see us, so..."

"So you *haven't* come up with an answer...," she concluded.

He rushed to protest. "N-no, I didn't say that. I've still got the secret trick up my sleeve!" he cried, pulling her by the hand down a riverside path to the left of the bridge. As the route to the castle grew farther away, she worried that he was about to suggest they swim across the river and climb up the rocky hill to sneak into the palace.

Kirito stopped at a spot where the river was wider, set the two bags on the ground, and looked up at Obsidia Palace again. The rocky black mountain was about three hundred mels across at the base but nearly twice as tall as that, so it looked more like a tower than a mountain. The majority of the side facing the city was carved into the shape of a castle, with majestic pillars and windows that gleamed in the morning sun. The rear side was still almost entirely raw mountain face, with just one large terrace jutting out, probably as a platform for dragons.

He lifted his right hand and pointed it at the top of the mountain. His finger twitched, as if he was searching for something.

"Um, Kirito...what are you...?" Ronie started to ask, feeling extra-apprehensive suddenly. He said nothing, holding his hand up another five seconds, then nodded as though he'd found the answer he wanted.

He lined up the fingers of that hand into a chopping position.

Then he lifted his arm straight up, pulled his left foot back, and dropped his center of gravity. The hand, upright like a sword, began to vibrate faintly and took on a white glow, to Ronie's shock.

Kirito hadn't spoken a word of any command. Which would mean this was the Integrity Knights' most secret power, a force that worked on the very laws of the world, Incarnation. But normally, it did not create any sound or light. How much power was he focusing to make it react this way?

"……*Hah!!*" he shouted, swinging the hand down with tremendous force.

White light shot forth in the form of a blade edge, much like Renly's Double-Winged Blades, instantly crossing over a kilor of space and hitting the handrail of a small terrace right at the top of the palace. With her excellent eyesight, Ronie could see little fragments of obsidian falling off the handrail.

"Wait…K-K-Kirito, what are you doing?! You just damaged the palace!!" she hissed, even more startled about that than the fact that he'd thrown an Incarnate Sword an entire kilor. She tugged his black cloak in a panic, but he got to his feet with practiced ease.

"That's nothing. Mix a little charcoal powder with glue and pack it on, and the marks will disappear…I think. Besides, look," he said, lifting his hand again to point. She could see a small figure emerging onto the distant terrace he'd just struck. It was too far away for them to make out its face, but the silhouette was slim enough that it was definitely a human. The person noticed the damage to the handrail, then leaned over the edge to look at the world below.

There was nowhere for Kirito and Ronie to hide on the riverbank, even if the palace was over a kilor away. The person on the terrace caught sight of them…it seemed.

The figure put a hand to its mouth.

Ronie only realized that the gesture was a whistle once a gray dragon spread its wings and took flight from the larger launching platform on the rear side of the mountain. The dragon rose as it rounded the side of the mountain, and then it hovered near the terrace in question. The figure hopped onto its back and pointed right at the side of the river where Ronie and Kirito stood.

"Th-th-that's b-b-b-bad news! They've completely spotted us!!"

"That was quick. Very sharp."

"I don't think this is the time for idle admiration! We need to get moving, or..."

But her tugging on his cloak proved futile. Kirito grabbed Ronie's arm and stood her in front of him instead. The dragon was now plunging downward, directly toward them.

Well, I guess I have to do my duty as bodyguard! she told herself, squeezing the hilt of her newly acquired longsword.

Just three seconds later, the gray dragon reached the space overhead and beat its wings to control its descent, and the rider hopped nimbly off its back, landing on the rocky riverside without a sound. Like the two of them, it was wearing a hooded cloak that kept its face hidden from sight.

The person wore no sword, but based on their mastery of the dragon, they must have been an elite dark knight. Ronie stood before Kirito, maintaining maximum vigilance to ensure that she was ready to draw her sword at any moment.

But...

The gray dragon landed after its rider, the ground shaking beneath their feet, and extended its long neck to sniff first Ronie, then Kirito. Then it trilled, soft and friendly, and nuzzled Kirito's head with the side of its long snout.

"Huh...?" Ronie was stunned. She'd heard that the dragons of the Dark Territory, like those back home, were very proud and standoffish with strangers. It was impossible for one to let down its guard this way around a stranger...But then she noticed the many lance scars on the dragon's gray scales.

"Oh...is that...?"

But Kirito answered the question before she could get it entirely out of her mouth. He rubbed under the chin of the dragon with both hands and said, "There, there. Good to see you again, too, Yoiyobi. How have you been?"

She would never forget that name. It belonged to a legendary dragon who'd fought bravely on its own against an army of red knights in the War of the Underworld. It was the partner not of a soldier of darkness, but of an Integrity Knight—a person who was another legendary figure, the Silent Knight...

"...Is...is that you...Lady Sheyta?" Ronie asked the hooded soldier.

The figure lowered its hood and said, "Kirito...Ronie. What are you doing here?"

Sheyta Synthesis Twelve.

Among the current state of the knighthood, she was one of the oldest knights after Fanatio and Deusolbert, and according to rumor, her skill with the sword was equal to that of the original commander, Bercouli Synthesis One.

Her divine weapon had been a gift from the pontifex herself. The Black Lily Sword could cut anything in the world, and Sheyta had used it to great effect against the hordes of pugilists and red knights in the war, in a true battle of one against many. But once the war was over, she had left Central Cathedral; now she lived in Obsidia Palace as the ambassador plenipotentiary for the council.

In other words, she was the perfect person for Kirito and Ronie to make contact with—the only problem had been how Kirito would summon her to meet them. The fact that he'd thrown an Incarnate Sword at the castle and the one person they'd needed had come out to investigate seemed more like a planned outcome than a lucky happenstance.

Ronie suppressed her desire to interrogate Kirito, choosing to observe their interaction with bated breath instead.

"I'm sorry to startle you like this, Sheyta," Kirito apologized, lowering his hood and scratching his head in embarrassment. It was the only idea I could come up with to get your attention..."

The faintest look of chagrin crossed Sheyta's reserved, beautiful features. "Yes, you did startle me. When I realized that someone had hit the edge with a blade of Incarnation from across the river, I thought that Commander Bercouli had come back to life."

Her manner of speaking was simple and flat, with none of the daintiness of her sex, but she was wordier than she had been in the past, and the tone of her voice felt softer somehow.

"...But how did you know that I was in that room?" Sheyta asked.

Kirito shrugged. "Because it felt the most dangerous, I guess."

Sheyta repeated his gesture, looking a bit disgruntled. "I thought that I was shutting off my sword spirit. If you can sense me from such a distance, then I still have much improvement ahead of me."

This told Ronie at last that Kirito hadn't been simply guessing about the target of his Incarnate Sword. The gesture he had made with his fingers before the light appeared around his hand must have been him searching for Sheyta's presence. It was a skill that she knew she could never replicate. But...

"Um, Kirito, if you have such incredible powers, did you really need to engage in what is essentially a child throwing a pebble at his friend's window?" she interjected.

Kirito turned to her and grinned. "What's this? Have you been visited by a boy like that before?"

"I—I wasn't speaking from personal experience!"

"Then maybe you were the one using it to—"

"N-no, of course I've never done anything like that!" she protested vigorously.

Sheyta gave them a thin, wry smile and then said to Ronie, "The long journey must have been tiresome. You may rest in the castle."

She gestured with her hand, and Yoiyobi lowered its body. There was no saddle on the dragon's back, but that meant there was enough room for the three of them to squeeze on together.

With Ronie in front, Kirito in the rear, and Sheyta sitting

between them, the veteran dragon took a quick run along the riverbank and gracefully took off, easily handling the weight of three people and two divine weapons.

With a powerful beat of its wings, the dragon rose rapidly, heading for the top of Obsidia Palace. The guards must have noticed by now, but they would know that it was the ambassador's dragon, and they hadn't raised an alarm about the scene.

Within two minutes, Yoiyobi brought them to the terrace, lowered the trio, then cried and returned to the larger platform on the other side of the mountain. When the huge creature was out of sight, Ronie walked over to the obsidian handrail to inspect the location Kirito had struck with his Incarnation. As she feared, there was a chunk over a cen deep missing from the feature.

That's going to get us yelled at, she thought, looking away—but when she actually glanced down at the sight before her, that brief concern of hers was entirely forgotten.

"Oh…wow…!"

Below her was the entire city of Obsidia. Unlike Centoria and its orderly, radial patterns, this was a city of chaos and disorder, but that just made it seem even more bold and alive.

"Over there, that looks like the ground itself is stacked up in several layers…Oh, and is that a coliseum? It's huge—Kirito, look!" Ronie said, pointing with excitement.

Over her shoulder, Sheyta said, "There are many other things to see here, and if you have the time, I would recommend some sightseeing…but on the other hand…" She turned away from Ronie and gave Kirito a piercing glance. "I assume you didn't sneak out to visit for fun. Has something happened in Centoria?"

"That's right," Kirito confirmed. He snapped to attention. "Ambassador Plenipotentiary Sheyta, I request an urgent meeting with Commander Iskahn."

The room leading to the terrace was full of warm, bright light, by the standards of the dark realm. The walls and ceiling were painted a pale pink, the curtains were pale yellow, and the rug was the green of fresh grass. The large fireplace burned rocks instead of firewood, and it was warm enough that if Ronie kept her cloak on, she might break into a sweat.

It was a surprising choice of decoration if this was Sheyta's room, she thought, but the real answer became apparent to her very quickly.

There was a small bed about a single mel long on the far side of the fireplace, and as Sheyta walked over to it, there was a stunningly warm and gentle smile on her face. She turned and beckoned Ronie and Kirito over in silence. They snuck closer and peered at the bed, where a baby wrapped in a pure-white blanket was sleeping soundly.

It was no more than three months old, with a tuft of soft hair that was dark red; its nose, mouth, and the hands clutched beside its head were all so tiny it was hard to believe.

According to the stories, this baby was the child of Sheyta and Iskahn, the leader of the pugilists guild. It was a girl, as Ronie recalled. She whispered to the mother, "What is her name...?"

"Leazetta," Sheyta said with a note of pride. She looked at Kirito and added, "I got the first syllable from the Green Swordswoman, Leafa."

"You did...? I had no idea," murmured Kirito, smiling as he gazed down at the sleeping infant.

A gentle, comforting silence filled the next twenty seconds, only to be broken by the sound of the door to the hallway swinging open and the world's worst example of a nasal baby-talk voice gushing forth.

"Lea, it's time for your yummy-nummy *miiilk*..."

A young man carrying two trays entered the room. His short curly hair, the golden-red color of fire, was held in place by a simple headband made of silver, and despite the winter season, he wore only a thin linen shirt. He sported short pants and sandals, but the rippling muscles and countless scars visible on his exposed shoulders and arms, along with his gouged-out right eye, indicated that he was a battle-hardened warrior.

In contrast, however, the slackened, goofy smile on that warrior's face was many times more blissful than even Kirito's expression when eating a honey pie. It left Ronie aghast.

The one-eyed man eventually noticed Ronie and Kirito standing near the bed, and his smile faded. His thick brows curled upward with suspicion, and his eyes glanced back and forth between them and Sheyta.

Before the man said anything, Kirito raised his hand and said, "Hey, Iskahn. It's been a while."

The supreme commander of the Dark Territory and champion of the pugilists guild, Iskahn, flared his one eye as wide as it could open. "Is…is that K-K-Kirito?! Why is your face colored like that…? I mean, what are you *doing* here?! The next meeting isn't until March!"

"Actually, I had a bit of an errand to run. Sorry to barge in on you without notice."

"W-well, that's all right…but hang on. Wait, wait, wait." A deep furrow ran through Iskahn's forehead. Sheyta slid over to her husband and took the trays from his hands. The pugilist seemed not to even notice it, he was so lost in his thoughts. "Kirito, did you…did you just hear that…?"

"Hear what…? Oh, about the yummy-nummy milk? You've really taken to fatherhood, haven't you? Ha-ha-ha."

"Don't you 'ha-ha-ha' me! Now that you've heard that, I can't let you leave unharmed. I've gotta pound that memory right outta your head!" he shouted, clenching his powerful fist, the skin glowing with pale-red flames.

"Um, K-K-K-Kirito…?" stammered Ronie, unsure of how to fulfill her role as bodyguard in the moment. He held out a hand to push her back and stood before Iskahn, thrusting out his left palm.

"Bring it!!"

"Raaaah!!"

Iskahn leaped. He left a red burning trail in the air, launching a punch with such speed that Ronie couldn't follow it with the naked eye. It made contact with Kirito's palm.

There was an explosive impact that sent the curtains and other decorative cloths swaying. It was clearly a devastatingly powerful punch, but Kirito stayed in place with no more than a slight backward lean, stopping Iskahn's blow with his one hand.

The pugilists' leader and the human realm's swordsman delegate went still, right and left hands connected. Eventually, Iskahn raised his head and smiled. "Good to see you haven't lost your touch, Kirito."

"Same to you, Iskahn."

Beside the men smiling creepily at each other, Sheyta held the trays with ill-disguised irritation. Ronie approached the bed, wondering if the sound had woken the baby. Instead, Leazetta was happily sleeping away without any notice of the clamor that had just happened. She really was the child of the strongest knight and pugilist in the world.

When the guards came, drawn by the sound of the blast, Iskahn pushed them back through the doorway and instructed them to bring two more chairs, which joined the two already lined up by the window. The guards were wary of Kirito and Ronie, of course, but they relented when Iskahn told them not to worry and that he would explain later. That was the effect of either the Law of Power or the trust Iskahn engendered as a leader.

After the guards left, the nine o'clock bells rang, and the baby awoke as if on command, scrunching up her face and crying. Sheyta scooped Leazetta up from the bed and sat down in one of the chairs to give her milk from a bottle fashioned out of phibo-tree nuts, which existed in the human realm as well.

When heated, phibo nuts became as translucent and hollow as glass bottles, and the nipple-like stem even had just the right amount of resiliency and perforation to allow liquid to pass through. For that reason, it was said that Terraria had created the plant precisely for babies. Now that Ronie knew about the real world, it was hard not to take that statement literally—that they really had been created, just by real-worlders, not Terraria.

Sheyta, in a trance, watched Leazetta drink noisily, then lifted her head and said, "Would you like to hold her?"

"May I?" Ronie asked.

"Of course."

She took the baby with her left arm and the bottle with the right and moved it to the baby's mouth. Leazetta's eyes stared at Ronie, gray like her mother's, but she resumed drinking the milk at once. Ronie had given Berche milk just like this several times at the cathedral, but holding a baby girl felt very different.

"I would have liked to nurse her myself, but the pugilists have their own secret mixture of milk formula," Sheyta explained.

Iskahn sensed the comment and turned away from his conversation about the latest news with Kirito to say, "You bet. If she drinks the formula, she'll never get sick, her bones will grow hard, and she'll be a good, strong child."

The term *milk* in the case of this mixture was an ordinary sacred word—a term that did not originate from the common tongue but was understood by all—and referred to cow's or goat's milk heated to skin temperature and mixed with certain medicinal elements specifically for infants. What that mixture consisted of varied by family and region—thus, Sheyta's reference to the secret formula. Ronie often heard that mother's milk was best, as Sheyta had said, and perhaps it was true, but if it weren't for phibo-nut bottles and milk mixture, it would be far more difficult for busy farming and merchant families to raise babies.

For her part, Leazetta had no complaints about the pugilists guild's secret recipe, and she drank it down in short order, then burped. She still looked sleepy, so Sheyta took her back from Ronie and laid her down in the bed again.

When she returned and sat down in the chair, her expression had gone from that of a mother to that of a knight.

"So what happened?" she asked, all business.

Kirito proceeded to tell them about the murder that had occurred two days earlier in South Centoria. Iskahn and Sheyta listened in silence, but when the story reached the topic of Oroi, the mountain goblin and murder suspect, they both inhaled. But they did not interrupt, so Kirito continued the story, explaining how he and Ronie had used a "dragon" to fly out of the human realm and reach Obsidia the night before.

"...I see...That's a hell of an ordeal we've put you through," said the commander, but the delegate just shook his head.

"No, I just wish I could have sent a messenger to warn you first...but I knew that it would be next month before they got an answer and completed the return trip."

Contact between Centoria and Obsidia at the moment happened through horse-bound messengers who traveled between a series of ten towns and forts. The entire process took a whole two weeks to get from one end to the other. And that wasn't even taking into account the danger of the many larger magical beasts that lived in the Dark Territory and might attack the messengers.

"True...If only we could find that master skull...," grumbled Iskahn, eliciting an understanding nod from Kirito.

So it fell to Ronie to ask, "Um, what's a...master skull?"

"Oh, that. I didn't know about it until after the war, either. During the War of the Underworld, Emperor Vecta used a Divine Object to give orders to Iskahn and the rest of the ten lords. It was a big master skull and ten slave skulls that went together. When he spoke into the master, his voice would instantly come out of the subsidiaries, no matter how far away they were."

His explanation left her wide-eyed. "I-instantly...?! If we had such a thing, there would be no need for letters or messengers at all."

"No, there wouldn't...But it's a one-sided conversation from master to slave, so you couldn't actually go back and forth with just that one set," Kirito noted.

"But after the war, the master skull and several of the slaves went missing, so even that much is out of grasp for now," Iskahn explained, exhaling deeply and shaking his head. "But the bigger problem is this murder in the human realm. It's impossible... The people who go on vacation in the human realm have to take a document forbidding theft, fighting, and killing, in the name of the Dark Council of Five and myself, supreme commander of the Dark Army. I sign every last one of those...so as long as the Law of Power exists, there's only one person in the entire dark realm who can ignore those orders."

Ronie assumed that he was speaking about himself, of course. But then Sheyta interjected, "Two people."

"......Only two people," Iskahn corrected himself, scowling. The corners of Kirito's mouth curled upward briefly.

"I agree with you," he said. "As a matter of fact, the dagger Oroi supposedly used to kill the human housekeeper vanished from the armory. I think it was most likely a temporary weapon, generated with steel elements...though that was Ronie's suspicion, not mine."

"Sounds like your pupil's got a good head on her shoulders."

"Sh-she's not a pupil, really...," Kirito said awkwardly.

Ronie began to wonder exactly *what* she was to Kirito, but she pushed the thought out of her mind and raised her hand to say, "Um, I was thinking a little more about that...The murder weapon was a re-creation of a mountain goblin dagger that was realistic enough for Oroi to mistake it for the real thing for a moment. So we've been assuming the whole time that a dark mage was involved in the incident somehow. But..."

She paused momentarily, looking at Sheyta and Iskahn in turn, and summoned up her courage to ask, "On that note, what is the state of the dark mages guild now...?"

Husband and wife shared a quick glance. Iskahn cleared his throat and answered, "I was going to report on this at the next meeting...Regrettably, we don't have a clear idea of the current state of the guild."

"What does that mean?" Kirito asked, his brows knit.

"After the Green Swordswoman slew Dee Eye Ell, a mage by the name of Kay Yu Vee took over. But though I don't know much about dark arts, even I could tell that she did not have the strength to maintain the guild," Iskahn said.

Sheyta added for clarity, "Even my skill with such arts is higher than hers."

"Upon further investigation, we found that when Dee was still alive, Kay was, at most, tenth in the internal hierarchy. Meaning that a whole bunch of the senior membership up and vanished."

"...Didn't nearly two thousand dark mages die in the battle at the Eastern Gate? Wouldn't that suggest they were in that group?" Kirito pointed out.

Iskahn scowled. "I doubt it...They're as tenacious as magical beasts when it comes to clinging stubbornly to life. If Dee hadn't fought with the Green Swordswoman, she'd still be alive today. They're not considerate enough that the top-ten mages would just up and die in battle together."

He looked back to Ronie and concluded, "So it's possible that the dark mages guild currently taking part in the Council of Five is just an empty shell. The real strength of the mages might be in hiding somewhere. And that means they might have had a hand in this trouble in the human realm. But...Ronie, was it? You seem to think differently."

"That's right. I don't have the evidence to completely deny that possibility...but I did think it was strange. If the real culprit is the dark mages guild in hiding, why would they need to create a false weapon from steel elements? Wouldn't they have been able to get a real goblin dagger pretty easily...?"

"...That's a good point. To a goblin, a dagger with their clan symbol on it is a pretty important item, but they're still mass-produced cast-iron pieces. You could easily come up with one or two by stealing or buying them from the right person," Iskahn muttered.

"If the true culprit's aim is to frame Oroi for the murder and escalate tensions between the two realms, having a real dagger would be a more effective method," Kirito agreed. "So if they weren't able to do that, would it mean that the culprit is...someone on the human side...?"

"That would raise an even bigger mystery," Sheyta pointed out, and her almond eyes narrowed even further. "On the human side, we are bound by far stricter laws than in the dark realm. Murder is a very clear violation of the Taboo Index. So if the person who killed the housekeeper is from the human realm, that would mean they are capable of ignoring the Taboo Index."

Kirito and Ronie nodded together in silence. That point had been raised in the discussion with Fanatio after the incident as well. Even an Integrity Knight unbound by the Taboo Index could not simply take the life of an innocent citizen like Yazen the housekeeper entirely of their own volition.

"We just don't know anything for sure," Kirito murmured, slowly shaking his head. Iskahn bobbed his head, lost in thought. Eventually, he clapped his hands, cutting through the figurative fog surrounding them.

"All right! We understand the situation now. Unfortunately, we'll probably need to cancel the sightseeing travel business to the human side for a time…"

"Yeah…We're keeping a lid on the information within Centoria for the time being, but if a second or third incident occurs, even the Unification Council won't be able to control the situation. I plan to temporarily close off the Eastern Gate and have the visitors currently staying in Centoria return home as soon as possible," Kirito said, with deep regret. "Also…as for Oroi the mountain goblin…We're keeping him in Central Cathedral for now, but we can't let him go right away. He might be able to give us more information, and we might be able to find out why he was framed. Oroi's from the Ubori clan on Saw Hill. I'm afraid that…"

"I understand. I'll send an envoy to the Ubori to explain the situation," Iskahn agreed. He turned his one eye to the window, then looked back at Kirito. "That settles the matter of the tourists going to the human realm…but what about the traders coming here from your side? There's a caravan of them staying in Obsidia at the moment."

"Hmm, that's a good question…," said Kirito, folding his arms. As part of the cultural exchange between the two sides, in addition to tourists visiting the human realm from the dark realm, the human side sent its own trading caravans to Obsidia. It was on a test scale for now, with just a few wagons' worth of goods selected for trading to see what worked and what didn't, but there were many exotic things here that couldn't be found inside the human realm, like those illumination ores. The bigger merchants could smell a major opportunity for business in the making, and they were pounding down the door with applications to be part of the caravans.

"...If the responsible party is an organizational power and it has members here in Obsidia, then they could be looking to cause the reverse of the human-killing...Say, one of the human traders killing a resident of Obsidia. But the caravans have veteran men-at-arms and arts-users as personal guards, and they're not allowed to wander around freely, either...so it wouldn't be that easy, I'm thinking," Kirito explained.

Sheyta agreed. "I don't think there's any need to cancel the trading business—not right away, at least. The caravans are bringing many valuable medicines and reagents here, so their presence is more welcomed than I might have thought...Just in case, I'll put a pupil on the caravan while they're staying in Obsidia."

"P-pupil...? I thought you were here on a solo assignment, Sheyta...," Kirito remarked, his darkened face wide with surprise.

With a mixture of concern and pride, Iskahn said, "That's the thing. Sheyta's currently both the ambassador plenipotentiary *and* a guest master of the dark knighthood."

"Wh-what does guest master mean...?"

"When she went to observe the knights, their young captain challenged her to a sparring match, so she used a borrowed sword—and not even the actual sword, just the scabbard—and beat him raw. Now she's got her own training hall at the knights' headquarters."

"I only have a handful of pupils; less than ten. But they've all got great potential," Sheyta explained.

"Ah...I see...," said Kirito, who was clearly at a loss for words.

She added, "You should come to the hall and give them a good demonstration."

"Oh, uh, g-gosh, I've barely trained in the traditional styles of swordplay at all…," Kirito mumbled, trying to edge away *with* the chair.

Iskahn reached out and clasped his shoulder. "That's perfect. After the knights, you can come to the pugilists' training hall, too. There are plenty there who doubt your true ability, and I need you to show them the Law of Power."

"I-I'd rather not! I've changed my mind; I want to be a bureaucrat!"

Oh dear…I don't think he's getting out of this one, thought Ronie, enjoying Kirito's panic.

Kirito and Ronie used Sheyta and Iskahn's private bath to wash off the dust of their travel, as well as their faces, and were taken to guest rooms on the same floor of the palace. Their unannounced visit was explained to the rest of the staff as an urgent envoy party.

It was not mentioned that Kirito was the swordsman delegate of the human realm, so the guards eyed his light armor with suspicion—envoys weren't typically armed—but they changed their attitude when they noticed the weapons the two carried. Divine Objects were even rarer in the Dark Territory than they were in Centoria.

They took a short rest in the two adjacent guest rooms, then joined Iskahn and Sheyta for lunch in the afternoon. They were guided around Obsidia to the headquarters of the dark knighthood and the pugilists guild by carriage in the afternoon. Kirito was nearly placed into a match with the massive, one-armed deputy captain of the pugilists guild but just barely managed to argue his way out of it by claiming, "I'm only on secret assignment!"

After that, they visited the central market and the great coliseum, but of course, the entire day wasn't just about sightseeing. Kirito and Iskahn spent much of the trip exchanging opinions about the incident and the cultural-exchange business, and Ronie was ever vigilant in her duty as a bodyguard. Of course, with the elite Integrity Knight Sheyta the Silent along, it was unlikely that Ronie's services would be necessary.

At that point, a thought belatedly occurred to her. When Sheyta had flown down on Yoiyobi, and over the course of their trip through the city, she hadn't been wearing a sword. As the carriage trundled back toward the palace, Ronie shifted down the long bench in Sheyta's direction.

"Um, Lady Sheyta? You don't have a sword with you...?"

The knight's eyes narrowed briefly with fond reminiscence. "No. The Black Lily Sword was my first and last blade."

"..."

Ronie still couldn't quite fathom what it meant for an Integrity Knight to lose the divine weapon that their heart and soul was fused with. She had no follow-up question, so Sheyta touched Ronie's hand reassuringly and smiled. "I am no longer Silent. I am Sheyta the Unarmed. And I am very pleased about that... although there are times that I recall the Black Lily and feel lonely."

"Oh...I see..."

I could never imagine the distant heights she inhabits, the apprentice realized in that moment.

Then it was Sheyta's turn to ask an unexpected question. "Did you just get that sword?"

"Y-yes...that's right. I haven't given it a name yet," Ronie admitted. She traced the silver hilt.

"I see. Your ties to it are shallow still, but it is a very good sword. Treasure it...because wars might end, but a knight's battles never do."

"Yes, ma'am!" Ronie said crisply. Across from them, Kirito and Iskahn looked over in surprise.

Eventually, the carriage passed through the castle town and crossed the bridge to the gate that was the official boundary of Obsidia Palace.

Standing at five hundred mels, the palace was a far cry from Central Cathedral's height but was still fifty stories, all told. It did not, however, have an automated levitating platform to transport people up and down. The stairs were the only means of getting to the upper levels, but it was said that this also served as a counter-measure against attacks.

The four of them climbed without stopping to the forty-ninth floor, where Iskahn and Sheyta lived. Kirito and the married couple were not fatigued by the trip, but Ronie was breathing heavily for a minute or two after they stopped—a sign that she had further physical improvements to make.

She thanked the three of them for waiting while she collected her breath, but then she noticed that the great staircase contin-ued farther upward. "Um...Lady Sheyta, what is above us?"

It was the supreme commander, not the ambassador plenipo-tentiary, who answered the question. "The fiftieth floor is the throne room. I've only gone in once or twice, though."

"Throne room...? For the emperor?" Kirito asked.

Iskahn scowled and nodded. "That's right. When Emperor Vecta appeared a year or so ago, it happened on the floor right above us."

"C-can we go and see...?" he asked, curiosity written on his face. Iskahn threw out his hands.

"I'd offer, of course...but the moment Vecta died—the moment you killed him—the door to the fiftieth floor was locked up by the Chains of Sealing again, and there's nothing you can do to sever them. There's a legend that says you can see the End Moun-tains and Eastern Gate from the fiftieth floor, so I wish I could go in again..."

The Integrity Knight of whom it was said there was "nothing she couldn't cut" nodded severely. "I borrowed a sword from the treasure repository to test it out, and I couldn't cut the chains. I could've done it in one swing with the Black Lily Sword, however."

"Hmm..."

It was clear to Ronie from the look on Kirito's face that he really wanted to try it with the Night-Sky Blade, so she quickly tugged on his sleeve twice. He picked up the mental *Don't you dare!!* signals from her and backed down, but not before one last longing look at the staircase.

"All right. Guess I'll have to forget about seeing the throne room."

"I'll make it up to you, though: We'll put together a dinner of all sorts of stuff you've never eaten before."

"That sounds fun," Kirito agreed.

Sensing the conversation was over, Sheyta took a step backward. "I'm going to give Leazetta her milk now. I'll see you at dinner."

"Oops, I've got to go with you. I've only seen my little girl's face once today."

The two new parents headed off. Kirito waved at them as they went, then took another glance at the stairs to the top floor. Ronie just shook her head in silence.

"I know, I know," he said, smirking. "C'mon...Let's go back to our rooms."

8

Dinner was just between Iskahn, Sheyta, Kirito, Ronie, and Leazetta, but it was a pleasant, lively evening, as though Ronie were back home in North Centoria.

Iskahn brought out exotic dishes, some of which almost seemed like pranks, such as rainbow lizard skewers and deep-fried sparking shrooms, but Kirito devoured them all with gusto, often screeching at the culinary results, much to Leazetta's cackling delight. The sight of their daughter enjoying herself left Sheyta and Iskahn beaming.

Ronie finished her meal with a newfound appreciation for the warmth of infants and families. She took her second bath of the day and headed back to her guest room.

The bath was much smaller than the one at Central Cathedral, of course, but considering that it was nearly at the top of a palace five hundred mels tall, it was nothing short of a miracle that there was fresh hot water available around the clock. It didn't seem to involve sacred arts, like at the cathedral, so it was quite a mystery as to how they were able to get so much hot water there in the first place. Afterward, she learned that when this had still been just an untouched mountain, hot spring water emerged near the top, and in the process of carving out the palace, the builders had utilized that water vein for the kitchen, baths, and internal heating.

The room was warm, and the bed was soft, compared to the cheap inn where they had stayed the night before, so Ronie changed into the nightclothes she was offered and grew sleepy before the nine o'clock bells. They'd be returning to the human realm in the morning, so an early bedtime was good, but a part of her didn't want the day to end. She lay on her side, facing the north wall.

On the other side of it, Kirito would be getting ready for bed. Perhaps he was already asleep. They'd been together for over forty hours since leaving Centoria, but it felt like she hadn't been able to tell him anything important to her yet.

The truly important thing was her duty to guard him, of course—she wasn't here so she could chat with him. Nevertheless, she had to desperately fight the urge to get out of bed and go knock on his door.

Kirito already had a partner: Asuna. She was a real-worlder like him, as beautiful as Stacia and kind to everyone, but as strong as could be when she drew her blade. In the war, Ronie could only huddle in the wagon and tremble, but Asuna had fought desperately to protect Kirito, suffering tremendous wounds in the process. Ronie didn't have the right to compete with someone like her.

I can't tell him how I feel. Never.

She pulled the thin blanket up to her head and shut her eyelids tight. But the sleepiness she'd allowed to slip away from her did not want to return.

Due to the exhaustion of the long trip, however, Ronie did eventually fall asleep without even extinguishing the ore lamps—until she was awakened by the sound of distant shouting.

Darkness lay outside the window; her body told her that it was probably two or three in the morning. She focused on her hearing without moving from bed and was about to close her eyes again and chalk it up to a dream when she heard the sound again. It was clearly a very tense, heated voice coming from beyond the door. There were several sets of rushing footsteps.

She got out of bed in her pajamas and pressed her ear to the door. The footsteps, presumably belonging to guards, faded away in the direction of the stairs, so she quietly opened the door and saw that Kirito was poking his head out of his room at the same time.

"What do you suppose they're shouting about?" she asked as the drowsy delegate trotted over to her.

"I don't know…but it sounds like the guards all rushed to the floor below us…," he mumbled, blinking until he was fully awake. He draped his cloak over her shoulders and said, "We should go check it out."

"Um…are you sure?"

"We might be able to help them with something," he said, patting her on the shoulder.

"Fine…but if we're only going to be in the way, then you have to come right back with me!" she cried out as Kirito started running down the hallway.

There was another shout, much clearer and louder, right as they reached the forty-eighth floor. "Get back!" said a voice that was unmistakably Iskahn's. Kirito and Ronie shared a look and rushed south down the wide hallway.

When the passage split at the end, they took the right fork and saw a large set of double doors. Whatever function this room served, it was an important one; the heavy obsidian doors were decorated with fine silver trim. They'd been thrown open, and shouts of fear and revulsion from the guards poured out.

Kirito and Ronie rushed down the last twenty mels of hallway and into the chamber.

Countless dazzling sources of light assaulted their vision on either side as they did, briefly blinding them. The ten or so guards farther in were holding ore lanterns that reflected off countless weapons, pieces of armor, jewels, and other items filling the large room. This had to be the armory—or perhaps the treasure repository—of Obsidia Palace.

"You monsters!" shouted Iskahn, his voice coming from the other side of the guards.

Kirito drew his sword and leaped cleanly over the throng of guards, vanishing beyond them. Ronie had no choice but to follow his lead, getting a short running start before jumping, cloak whipping over her nightwear.

In addition to the characteristic consecutive techniques of Kirito and Asuna's Aincrad-style swordfighting, the two of them placed heavy emphasis on quick steps and big jumps, tactics that Ronie was working hard to master. Thanks to that, she was just able to clear the group of guards. She heard them shout with surprise behind her, but there was a more pressing matter that occupied her attention now.

A few mels ahead of them were Iskahn and Sheyta, both in their nightclothes. And beyond them were two dark figures.

Monsters really was the only word to describe them. Their shape was similar enough to that of a human or demi-human, but their necks and arms were much longer, and their mouths were perfectly round circles with rows of inward-pointing fangs that stretched and contracted ceaselessly, like a certain species of fish. Four eyes lined each side of the elongated heads, wings of thin membrane grew from their backs, and a long tail dangled from each of their waists.

"Are those…minions?!" shouted Kirito. Sheyta and Iskahn glanced back at the sound of his voice.

"Sorry, guess we woke you up. But we can't let our own trouble spill over onto our guests! I'm gonna destroy those freakish things with one blow!!" bellowed Iskahn, clenching a fist that shone like fire. But Sheyta extended her hand to stop her husband.

"Minion blood is poisonous. You can't attack them barehanded."

"Yeah, but…," Iskahn protested. As if understanding the conversation and seizing on the moment of opportunity, the two minions hissed aggressively.

It was Ronie's first time seeing a minion, but she knew about them. They were artificial creatures that served the dark mages of the Dark Territory. Many of them had been summoned for the battle at the Eastern Gate at the start of the War of the Underworld, but the Perfect Weapon Control art of Commander Bercouli's Time-Splitting Sword had wiped the entire unit out. Since they hadn't actually done any damage to the human army, they had come off as little more than large bats, but in truth, they were much more horrifying than that. They stood nearly two mels tall, and the claws at the ends of their lanky arms were as long and sharp as knives.

They were also resistant to all kinds of elements, as well as thrusting and bludgeoning attacks. The most effective means of damaging them was a slash from a sharp blade, but Iskahn and Sheyta had no swords, of course. Too late to do anything about it, Ronie wished that either she or Kirito had brought the swords from their bedrooms.

"Supreme Commander, let us handle this!" shouted one of the guards behind them, but Iskahn refused to move.

Whatever orders the minions were under, they only made those threatening hissing sounds, without actually attacking. A number of shelves were toppled over to the sides of the creatures, and jewelry and accessories were spilled everywhere, but the monsters were not stealing them.

How were these creatures able to sneak into the treasure repository near the top of the palace without attracting any attention from the guards anyway? Ronie wondered.

She soon got her answer, however: The huge wings on their backs meant they had no need to climb up all those stairs. They had just blended into the dark of night and come in through a window. She glanced behind them and saw, on a distant wall, the broken metal frame of the window in question.

And if they could do that, then…then…

Thoughts exploded in Ronie's mind like sparks right as Kirito gasped beside her.

"Out of the way, you two!" he shouted, thrusting out his right hand. Pale light shone around his outstretched palm—thirty frost elements, all at once.

Sheyta and Iskahn leaped to the sides immediately. Kirito promptly shot the frost elements forward and unleashed them around the two minions. Ordinarily, simply unleashing frost elements would cause their effect to be diffused over a large area, but this chill blast clung only to the minions, as though shaped by some advanced arts, freezing the ink-black creatures with white ice.

"*Gshyaaaa!!*" the minions screeched, their long heads writhing, but soon even their mouths were frozen, stopping them cold. It was a tremendously powerful demonstration, but the minions had been created from clay and were hardy against flames and ice. Even frozen, they would not be suffering much damage as far as their lives were concerned...

But Kirito had an answer for this, of course. With his hand still outstretched, he commanded, "Now, you two!!"

"All right!!" shouted Iskahn triumphantly as he leaped. Sheyta followed his lead.

"Raaaah!!" His punch burst straight through the body of the minion on the right. Then Sheyta used the side of her hand as a makeshift blade to graze the left minion in a vertical descent.

A moment later, the right minion exploded into a million pieces, and the left minion split into two symmetrical halves. Because both of them were frozen solid, not a single drop of their toxic blood spilled.

The guards in the back cheered, and Iskahn turned around with an exasperated but impressed smile. "You're even crazier than the stories about you suggest, Kirito. I always heard that even for the most advanced of mages, five elements generated by a single hand was the maximum..."

"We can talk later, Iskahn!" Kirito said, interrupting his own praises. He sounded even more agitated now than he had when he was giving orders before. "The minions weren't trying to steal treasure or attack us. Whoever set them loose was just buying time!"

It was at that point that Ronie's previous flash of inspiration turned into tangible alarm. Sheyta's face went pale as well.

"Oh no...," she murmured, speeding off. Ronie and Kirito rushed through the guards like the wind and bolted out of the treasure repository.

"We'll go, too!" shouted Kirito.

Iskahn tightened his nightclothes, which were in the style of those worn in the eastern empire, and began to run, his bare feet slapping against the polished obsidian floor. "Wh-what do you mean?" he asked. "Diversion from what...?"

"I think whatever the mage is after is something far more precious than jewels," Kirito called back.

"Far more precious...?" Iskahn repeated. His eye suddenly shot open with alarm. Ronie almost imagined that she *heard* his reddish-gold hair standing on end.

"Leazetta," the pugilist gasped. His feet glowed a pale red.

He shot off the floor with a *bang!*, leaving it cracked like a spiderweb. He pulled away from the other two with superhuman speed and reached the stairs a few seconds behind Sheyta, who was in the lead. Iskahn bounded up to them, skipping four or five steps at a time, Kirito following right behind with smooth footwork.

Ronie ran as best she could, grappling with a fear that threatened to paralyze her body. She ascended the stairs and rushed into the corridor of the forty-ninth floor, but the other three were already out of sight. She only heard their distant footsteps.

She continued running after them, past the baby's room, which she'd been taken to when she first arrived at the palace, and to the room at the end of the hall, which was presumably the bedroom of the parents. She hurtled through the open doorway and found a hideous smell stinging her nostrils.

The room was dark, lit only by a single ore lamp, but the large, shattered window frame, the dark pool of blood in front of it, and the two collapsed guards were very clearly visible.

The miasmic pool of blood, which probably belonged to a minion, spread beneath the fallen guards. They were both breathing but groaning in agony, either from their wounds or from the effect of the poison. Only Iskahn was visible otherwise.

"Gude! Gaihol!" shouted Iskahn, casting toward them. "What happened?!"

One of the guards motioned for him to get back with a wave. "No, Commander, don't touch it..."

The other one grimaced, more out of bitter regret than pain. "A while after you two went down below, we heard the window breaking...and when we went inside, a black monster was there...We nearly managed to vanquish the creature, but all of a sudden, a dark mage was in the room, casting a charm of blindness on Gude and me..."

When the second guard stopped, panting, the first one continued the story: "We got covered in the monster's blood, and it sapped our ability to move. The mage picked up Leazetta from the bed and went out the window on the monster...and that's the last thing I saw..."

"......I see...," said Iskahn, audibly clenching his jaw.

On the right side of the room, there was a bed for two near the wall, with a small child's cradle on the other side. Leazetta must have spent the daytime in the bright, sunlit baby room before coming here at night to sleep with her parents.

That adorable baby, just three months old, had been kidnapped. It was such a horrible thought that Ronie was frozen with shock. Sheyta and Kirito returned to the room from the terrace on the other side of the broken window.

"...We can't find them. No response on the dark-element search art," Sheyta murmured quietly.

Kirito shook his head, too. "I couldn't sense anything, either," he said with chagrin. Then he turned to the guards collapsed on the floor and raised his hand, generating elements as he had in the treasure room. This time it was not the white of frost elements, but light elements. There were about ten of them, which he split into two groups and pressed against the guards' bodies.

A warm glow suffused the two, and the majority of the black liquid pooling on the floor simply vanished, as if evaporated by the light. The guards rubbed their own bodies with wonder, breathing heavily, and then bounced to their feet and bowed deeply to Sheyta and Iskahn.

"Commander, Ambassador, we are utterly shamed by our inability to fulfill our duty!"

"We were charged with protecting Leazetta with our lives, and now they must be forfeit as punishment..."

Iskahn reached out and grasped the shoulders of the two men. "None of that is going to return my daughter to me. I'd rather have your strength in the fight to take Leazetta *back*."

Despite the way his heart must have been torn to pieces, Iskahn kept his voice under control and lifted the men back to an upright position. "The first thing I want to know about is the appearance of this dark mage. Did you see a face? Hear a voice?"

"Well...," said the taller guard, the one named Gude. "The figure wore a black hood pulled low, hiding their face...I couldn't tell you any details about the mage's voice. I couldn't even tell if this person was a man or a woman..."

"I see..." Iskahn bit his lip.

Kirito picked up the questioning. "How many minutes passed between the mage escaping through the window and us coming back to the room?"

The heavier-set guard, Gaihol, answered, "Three...maybe only two minutes..."

"Two minutes...?" Kirito repeated, frowning. He looked out the window at the night sky.

Sheyta was taken aback by this, too. She murmured, "They rode on an injured minion and vanished in just two minutes...?"

According to what they taught in the dark-arts lectures at the Great Library, a minion's flight speed was equivalent to a human being's running speed. This was five hundred mels per hour in the air, so whatever the direction, it seemed impossible for them to be completely out of sight in just two minutes, but the dark mage could perhaps have used some kind of hiding charm. In any case, if Kirito and Sheyta couldn't find them, Ronie didn't stand a chance.

Racked with the feeling of futility, she crossed the room to the baby's bed. The cradle was empty, of course, except for an adorable pacifier and little bear and dragon plush toys. The sight tore her heart to pieces.

Ronie was pulling her gaze away from the bed when she happened to notice something strange had fallen onto the dragon plush toy. She reached out for it.

It was a sheaf of parchment, bound with red string. This clearly was not a child's toy.

"Um…I found this in the bed…," she said, holding out the parchment. Iskahn shot across the room like lightning to take it. He snapped the tough-looking string with his fingertips and opened it up. The pugilist's one good eye stared, and air rasped from his throat. He stumbled and sat down on the bed.

Sheyta snatched the paper away from him. Shock spread across the knight's features. She bit her lip and handed it to Kirito next. Ronie stood next to him so she could read the dark letters on the parchment.

By sundown on the twenty-first day of the second month, the Human Unification Council's swordsman delegate must be publicly executed in the great coliseum for the crime of an attempted assassination of the Dark Territory's supreme commander, and his head must be sent back to the human realm. If this requirement is not met, the head of an innocent babe will be delivered to Obsidia Palace.

"…N…no……"

Ronie shook her head again and again. The twenty-first day

was today. That meant they had only thirteen or fourteen hours until sundown, the deadline for the execution.

Her first thought was that Iskahn and Sheyta would never let Kirito be executed. But then she realized that their beloved newborn daughter's life was at stake. What could be more important to them?

Ronie reached down and brushed her left side without thinking. There was no sword to be found. Like Kirito, she had left her weapon in the bedroom.

And even if she had it on her person…if Iskahn and Sheyta did the unthinkable and followed the abductor's demands, could she actually fight them? If Kirito and Ronie ran away, Leazetta would die.

She couldn't imagine abandoning that sweet, innocent babe to this horrible fate. But it was also her duty as a bodyguard to protect Kirito; she couldn't allow him to be executed. It was the last thing she could do.

Ronie was conflicted like she'd never been before in her life. She wanted to look over at Kirito's face as he read the parchment, but she couldn't even budge her neck to turn.

"Um…my lord…," stammered Gude the guard, standing along the wall with his partner. He was probably curious about the contents of the parchment, but Iskahn just lifted a weary hand and pointed toward the door.

"Gude, Gaihol, go into the hall and do not let anyone inside."

"Yes, sir…"

They gave salutes in the Dark Territory's style, then headed for the door. Along the way, Gaihol stopped and turned back. "Um, there is one more thing to report…"

The four others turned to look at the squat guard, who hunched his short neck to appear even shorter.

"It's nothing especially important," he continued, "but…right after the dark mage and the monster left out the window, I felt like I heard a strange noise."

"Noise…? What kind?" Sheyta queried.

Gaihol opened and closed his mouth several times, searching for the right words. "It was like…a stone mortar and pestle turning, like a grinding sound…"

"Stone mortar and pestle…?" repeated Iskahn. He knew much about this castle, but it didn't seem to be a familiar idea to him. Gaihol saluted again, left the room with Gude, and closed the door.

A heavy silence filled the bedroom until Kirito said, "Iskahn, Sheyta…I'm sorry. It's my fault this has happened…"

"…What are you talking about? You're not responsible for this," snapped Iskahn from the bed, despite the fact that he must have been beside himself with worry. "It's my fault. I let Lea's guard be thinned out, and I fell right for that diversion. But… And I hate to make excuses, but the dark mages' minions aren't supposed to be able to fly to this height. Only the dragon riders of the dark knighthood can get this high, but they're forbidden from approaching any point but the landing platform around the back. So I just assumed that no one would be able to sneak through the window, coming after us…"

His hands clenched atop his knees to the point of cracking. Sheyta walked over to her husband and placed a slender hand on his.

"Even still, I'm the one who invited this situation," repeated Kirito, still holding the extortion letter. "Ronie recognized the possibility that the murder in the human realm could have been a trap to get me to travel to Obsidia. But I assumed that if I traveled to Obsidia in a single day, whatever conspiracy was being concocted couldn't catch up with me. The people who stole Leazetta were a step ahead of me, though…They had people in both lands, and they have a means of communication faster than a dragoncraft."

"Dragon…craft? And you can use that to travel from Centoria to Obsidia in a day?" Sheyta marveled.

"Yeah. I'll show it to you sometime. But your daughter comes first…," Kirito said. He looked at the parchment again and continued, "Their purpose, I presume, is to pit the human realm and dark realm against each other again. If we ignore them, they're certain to make good on their threat. I'm going to give everything I have to get Leazetta back...but if I fail to find her, then I want you to—"

"Don't say it!!" snapped Iskahn, preventing Kirito from saying *execute me.*

Ronie had heard from Kirito and Asuna before about the workings of how they traveled to the Underworld from the real world. They lay down to rest in a Divine Object of sorts called an Ess Tee Ell, which transported their souls, but only their souls, to the Underworld. Because of that, if they lost all their life value in the Underworld, they would not die. Their souls would return to the real world, where they would reawaken.

That was probably on Kirito's mind now. But if he went back to the real world, he most likely would never be able to return to the Underworld, according to the two of them. To Ronie—and to all the other people who had met Kirito and shared their time with him—that meant he might as well be truly dead. The human realm...the entire Underworld...still needed him.

She couldn't put words to the storm of thoughts and emotions running through her, so instead, Ronie took a step closer to Kirito and squeezed the sleeve of his black shirt. Sheyta saw her do it, and the corners of her mouth softened the tiniest bit. She nodded to Ronie to put her at ease.

"First I will go to the dark mages guild headquarters in the north district. I'm certain that it was an unaffiliated mage who burst into this room, but if the minions' formula has been improved somehow, we might be able to unravel the mystery from there."

"All right...I'll go with you. If it's just you, the damn mages might try to weasel their way out of telling the truth," said Iskahn, jumping to his feet and lifting the silver headband from the headboard of the bed so he could place it around his forehead. Sheyta tore off her nightclothes and started to change, which forced Ronie to hide her eyes with alarm.

Kirito, meanwhile, was looking out the broken window again. He bit his lip pensively, deep in thought. The couple was done changing by the time he turned back and said, "Is it possible that the mage and the minion who kidnapped Leazetta returned to the castle on a different floor?"

Iskahn scowled and grunted. "Hmm...All the windows are locked at this hour, and if they broke through one to get inside, the guards on that floor would notice...but if there's a mole in the palace, they could open a window to let them inside..."

Sheyta agreed with him and added, "We'll have all the guards search the entire palace."

"Can Ronie and I help with that?" Kirito requested. Iskahn agreed without hesitation.

"Please do. If there are more minions about, we'll need your power. Take this."

He opened a small drawer in the footboard of the bed, pulled out a silver necklace, and tossed it to Kirito, who caught it one-handed. Iskahn jabbed a thumb at his own headband. "This is the sign of the military's supreme commander, and *that's* the sign of his deputy. Show that and give them my name, and you can get away with just about anything."

"Got it. Thanks," Kirito said, placing the chain around his neck; from it hung a small silver pendant with a crest on it. Iskahn marched over to the swordsman with big strides and clasped Kirito's shoulder.

"...Please," he said simply, the only word that needed to be said. Then he turned and rushed out of the room with Sheyta. The door opened, then shut, and as if on cue, the bells for the four o'clock hour softly played their melody.

9

Kirito and Ronie returned to their rooms, changed into their normal gear—swords included—and began their search from the forty-ninth floor.

But they did not actually open every door and check every room. Kirito's Incarnation power was so strong that he could sense Sheyta's room from across the river, and he could detect the presence of people or monsters through the doors and walls, so simply concentrating from the center of the floor was enough to tell him what he needed to know.

Every time a guard told them off, he would show them the chain with the symbol of the supreme commander on it and move on. They spent two hours rushing from floor to floor, making their way down the castle.

At that point, Kirito was in the third basement floor, a massive storage space at the very bottom of Obsidia Palace. At a hallway intersection, he closed his eyes and focused—only to shake his head.

"Nope...not here, either." He sighed and leaned back against the black rock wall. The storage area was completely devoid of people; the only movement in the silent corridor was the weak flickering of the ore lamps.

Ronie asked her pensive partner, "So does that mean they're not in the castle...? Could they have escaped outside?"

"Yeah…But that would have to mean that the injured minion flew over three kilors in just two minutes…"

"Three kilors…? Is that how far you can sense?"

"It depends on the target, but in empty space, and tracking something as large as a minion, there's no mistaking it. So at a kilor and a half per minute, that would translate to ninety kilors an hour. I can't imagine that any minion can fly at such an extreme speed."

"It would be a dragon at that point…Do you think that the dark knighthood is involved somehow, then?" Ronie whispered.

Kirito shook his head again. "I can sense a dragon at ten kilors. And no dragon could fly that far in two minutes, though the dragoncraft might…"

He paused, mouthing the words *No way*, but then he ruled that out. "No…if they were using the dragoncraft, it would have created a tremendous sound. Nothing as quiet as a stone pestle grinding against a mortar. And…what would a stone mortar and pestle grinding sound like anyway…?" he wondered.

Ronie considered it but couldn't come up with a satisfactory answer. Instead, all she could envision was the warmth of Leazetta drinking milk in her arms, without a care in the world, and the way she squeaked and giggled during dinner. Ronie clutched her arms tight around herself.

"Leazetta is the hope that ties the two realms together," Kirito murmured. "We can't let her be killed. We just can't…"

The kernel of sheer determination buried in the midst of the deep concern in his voice took Ronie's breath away. Kirito was leaning back against the wall with his head down, out of sight. She walked over to him, as if in a trance, and grabbed his shoulders.

"…You can't, Kirito. You can't sacrifice yourself."

After a long silence, Kirito mumbled, "I told you before, remember? If I die in this world, I don't actually die. So it's better me than h—"

"No!" shrieked Ronie. "That logic doesn't apply…I…I'll never see you again. And I don't want that to happen…I don't!!"

She buried her face in his chest. The silver crest pendant bit into her forehead, but the pain in her skin was nothing next to the throbbing that gouged out her heart.

"I will be your page for life. I've decided that I'm going to serve at your side forever. I don't want anything else…but if you decide to make yourself a sacrifice, I will join you. I will force you to have me executed, too!"

It was unfair, turning herself into a hostage. But it was also the unvarnished truth of what she wanted at that moment.

"…Ronie…," he murmured, his voice full of anguish. He lifted his hands to grab her shoulders.

If he really wanted to, he could tie her in place or even knock her unconscious for two or three days—as long as it would take for everything to be over. But there would be no point. If he had been executed by the time she woke up, she'd simply follow him beyond the veil.

He reached up to stroke her hair and whispered, "Thank you, Ronie. I won't give up. I'll find a way to rescue Leazetta…and I'll return to the cathedral with you. That's our home…"

Tears flooded from her eyes. Her throat tensed up as she desperately tried to hold in the sobs that wanted to break free.

"…Yes……yes…," she managed to squeak, and she let her entire weight rest against Kirito. He continued to stroke her hair until she calmed down.

Ten minutes later, they returned to the ground floor of the castle as the six o'clock bells rang. Sheyta and Iskahn were returning from the dark mages guild headquarters at the same moment. They regrouped and shared information—sadly, none of it was directly related to the kidnapper.

"At the guild, they don't have a handle on the mages who went missing in the war, and they haven't been doing any experimentation on augmenting minions. I questioned them as the supreme commander, and by the Law of Power, they can't lie to me," Iskahn said.

Sheyta gloomily added, "There was one lead, however...About a month ago, at a clay-harvesting spot under the guild's control, a large amount of the finest clay that had already been extracted and bagged went missing."

"A large amount? Like...how much?" Kirito asked.

Iskahn scowled and said, "Around enough to make three minions, they said. They handled the incident internally and didn't report it to the Council of Five...Though I doubt we could have predicted this would happen today, even if we'd been aware of the theft..."

"A month ago...Then it probably does have something to do with the incident in Centoria," Kirito murmured.

"We already got the report from the guards...but how did *your* search go?" Iskahn asked.

"Well...we searched from the top floor to the storage all the way underground and didn't find any minions or Leazetta. It wouldn't even matter if there were hidden rooms or spaces you didn't know about. As long as they weren't hiding in some place completely isolated from consecutive space, they couldn't have evaded my searching ability."

"If you say it, then it must be true...Which would mean they have to be far, far away by now..."

Iskahn scratched at his silver-ringed head in desperation. Sheyta reached out to grab his hand and stop him, and she enveloped it with both of hers.

With silence filling the great hall, the sound of the main doors of the castle closing was loud and heavy. The doors, including the hinges, were carved from obsidian, which made the sound of all that rock scraping quite distinct, almost like the rumble of distant thunder. Ronie felt like she'd heard the sound not that long ago, and she searched her memories.

It was...Yes, it was during the test flight of Dragoncraft Unit One at Central Cathedral. In order to keep the craft from colliding with the top of the building, Asuna used Stacia's divine power to shift the top five stories of the building aside. The massive chunk of marble scraped against itself and made that sound.

Rock on rock...scraping. Like a mortar and pestle.

"...Oh! Um, Lady Sheyta...," she said, rushing over to the senior Integrity Knight, her mind a whirling blur. "Near your bedroom, is there another large obsidian door like the front gate here?!"

"Obsidian door...? No, all the doors around are wooden, and the window frames are iron."

"Are there any mechanisms that would involve stone scraping on stone...?"

That question got Kirito involved:

"Oh...! When the guards said they heard a sound like a stone mortar and pestle! Yes...if there's a hidden door on the exterior of the castle, it might make that kind of noise...but..."

"But if it was *just* a hidden door, your nose could sniff it out?" Iskahn finished. He crossed his arms. "Plus...I've never heard about anything like that near our bedroom. Besides, why would you put a secret door on the outside that no one can use? It wouldn't make sense unless you could fly."

"What if...it's not a secret door...?" Kirito muttered, looking up at the ceiling of the great hall. "You said it yourself, Iskahn. The *real* top floor is above the current top floor of the castle."

The commander and the ambassador gasped at the same time.

"The...the fiftieth floor...? B-but it's sealed airtight, and the guards saw that the chains weren't cut."

"What about from the outside? Is there even a single window on the fiftieth floor?"

"......Actually......actually...I think...," Iskahn murmured, craning his neck as he thought. "When Vecta appeared...and he summoned the ten lords, there *was* a huge window in the throne room. But now...when you look at it from the outside, there's just a solid rock face above the forty-ninth floor, without any window..."

"It must have closed up," Kirito said, absolutely certain now. "When Vecta died and the chains resealed the room, the stone outside must have moved to cover up all the windows. The space was completely cut off from the rest of the world. The stone-grinding sound the guards heard was the rock moving once again."

"But...but...," Iskahn stammered, his burnished skin going pale. "Only Emperor Vecta can undo the seal on the fiftieth floor...Would that mean the one who abducted Lea is...?"

He gritted his teeth, afraid of even finishing that sentence. A horrified silence followed, until Sheyta cut through it with a voice like a blade.

"Let's go to the fiftieth floor."

Kirito agreed. "Yes...We might learn something if we examine the door."

Iskahn nodded—anything to wipe away his trepidation.

The four rushed back to the top of the castle without a break once again. Ronie was able to keep up with them without running out of breath this time; perhaps she'd gotten the hang of the process.

The group stopped on the forty-ninth floor and looked up the last stretch of stairs. Either because the palace's internal heating system didn't extend that far or for some other reason, Ronie felt chilly air sweeping down the darkened staircase and clinging to her legs.

"...Let's go," Iskahn said, starting up the steps. The other three followed.

It was only one flight of stairs, but it felt even longer than the trip from the first floor to the forty-ninth. A set of pitch-black double doors met them at the top. As the pugilist had said, the doors were locked up with huge chains about ten cens thick. They were pulled absolutely tight, with virtually no give.

Iskahn walked slowly down the short hall to the doors, touched the gray chain, and pulled back, yelping, "It's cold!"

Determined, he reached out again and grabbed it fully. He crouched, shouted, and yanked on it, but the chain only made a slight clanking noise and did not budge.

"...So the seal's not broken..."

He let go of the chain and touched the black door this time, then used both hands, and even pressed his ear to the surface.

"I don't hear anything...but if Lea's anywhere inside the castle, it's got to be past here..."

The pugilist took a couple of steps back, paused a few moments, then assumed a fighting pose. Red flames curled from his clenched right fist. The chilly air began to vibrate, and Ronie's instincts told her to keep her distance.

Was he going to punch those chains with his bare fist? Kirito stepped forward at that moment, unaffected by the tremendous battle aura wreathing the pugilist's body, and placed a hand on his shoulder.

"I'll do it, Iskahn."

"No...let me do this."

"Save your fist for the fight against the minions and kidnappers. Plus, I'm good at this sort of thing," Kirito said simply. Iskahn exhaled, paused, and finally decided to undo his stance.

"You can get away with anything, can't you? Fine...it's all yours," he grumbled, standing back next to his wife.

Now it was Kirito who stood before the chains. His glowing hand delicately brushed the surface of the metal. After repeating the action a few times, he traced a spot in the center of the chain several times with a finger.

"Here...It's so shallow you can't see it, but there's a mark here. Did you do this, Sheyta?" he asked without turning around.

The Integrity Knight said, "Yes. As I said earlier, the Black Lily Sword could have cut through it."

"I bet...I'm going to use this mark now."

He let go of the chain and took three steps back, then squeezed the handle of his sword. When he drew it with a low sliding sound, Iskahn and Sheyta gasped in wonder.

The Night-Sky Blade was made not of metal but of a black material with just a trace of translucence. It looked much like the stone that Obsidia Palace was carved out of, but this smooth, heavy, wet-looking substance was not rock: It was carved from the branch of a gargantuan cedar tree that had once loomed over the forest at the northern edge of the Norlangarth Empire. Sadore, the old man who now ran Central Cathedral's arsenal, had spent an entire year and six whetstones honing the branch into a longsword. Kirito had used it to defeat several Integrity Knights, then Prime Senator Chudelkin and Administrator, and lastly, Emperor Vecta. It was quite literally the legendary sword that had saved the world.

But no matter how high the priority level of the sword, the weapon alone would not be able to cut the sealing chains. Those chains, like the exterior of Central Cathedral or the Everlasting Walls that split Centoria into four sections, possessed a characteristic that made them unbreakable. Even Asuna and her godly powers could only *move* the cathedral walls, not destroy them.

The thing that would sever these chains was not a swordsman's skill or a sword's power but the miraculous ability to overwrite the very laws of the world—Incarnation.

Kirito took three more steps back, held out his left hand, and pulled back the Night-Sky Blade in his right until it was at his shoulder. His feet gripped the floor, spread front and back. He took a deep breath and held it.

Red light glowed all over Kirito's body, which was now in a stance belonging to no traditional swordfighting style. A whirlwind kicked up from the floor, causing Ronie to look away, but she held her ground.

Eventually, the red light coalesced in the sword in his hand, turning the black blade crimson. There was a howling like the wind through branches, growing louder and louder, until it took on the metallic tinge of a dragon's roar. The air crackled and shuddered, and even the obsidian floor and walls began to shake.

"Un…believable…!" Iskahn exclaimed.

"This is all…Kirito's Incarnation…," Sheyta quietly marveled.

Suddenly, Kirito, dressed in a simple black shirt and trousers, was flickering like an illusion in the midst of a storm of light and air, such that he transformed—or at least, so it appeared. Perhaps the whipping-back-and-forth effect was just the hem of his black leather cloak. Steel armor shone on his shoulders and the right side of his chest.

"Raaah!!" he bellowed, pushing off the ground.

The sword in his hand thrust forward, bearing all his Incarnation. The roaring rose to an extreme level, and fine cracks appeared in the walls to their sides.

The distance to the chains was five mels, clearly outside the range of his sword. But as though the sword stretched and grew, the crimson light surged like a spear and penetrated a single spot on the chains that locked the doors.

Sound vanished, light vanished, wind vanished—and Kirito's appearance returned to normal.

In the ensuing silence, the length of chain split silently in two, dangling at the sides. The heavy doors seemed to shudder—or come back to life as doors—and groaned briefly.

Kirito fell to a knee on the floor. Ronie rushed to his side.

"Kirito!" She slipped an arm under his flank and helped him get up. Sheyta and Iskahn rushed over a moment later.

"Are you okay, Kirito?!" shouted Iskahn.

Kirito held up his free hand. "Yeah...I'll recover soon. Hurry, go through the door...before the system—er, before the laws of the world notice the abnormality and restore the chain."

"Good idea," said Sheyta, approaching the massive doors and pressing her hands against the menacingly carved obsidian slabs. They rumbled and gave way just the tiniest bit. "They're open," she announced, turning back.

"Hurry, you two!" the Black Swordsman commanded. "If the kidnapper's inside, they'll have noticed the doors are open now... I'll catch up in a moment!"

"G-got it!"

Iskahn smashed the doors open with a single kick. The hallway continued beyond the doorway, but it was filled with a darkness of a different kind than that over the stairs. Freezing-cold air poured forth.

But Leazetta's parents hurtled down the hallway without a moment of hesitation. A few seconds after they disappeared into the darkness, Kirito shouted encouragement and willed himself back to his feet. "Let's go," he told Ronie.

She suppressed her concern and replied, "Understood!"

It seemed like a good idea to call the guards currently searching downstairs before they rushed in, but Kirito was right: Every moment counted now. And if the enemy was an advanced user of dark arts, a few guards with a bit of sword training were only going to be targets, not a source of help.

Instead, she pulled out a little bottle of medicinal solution from her carrying bag, removed the stopper, and handed it to Kirito. He glugged it down and made a face at the bitter, sour taste, but his complexion was already looking ruddier as he thanked her. They lined up at the doorway and stepped into the dark passageway.

It felt like they had just passed through a transparent membrane. Chilly air surrounded them, turning their breath white, as though the interior heating system did not work here. But the cold and fear completely vanished when Ronie heard a noise from farther down the hall.

The sound of a baby crying.

"...!"

She and Kirito shared a look and took off running.

The passage turned left up ahead. Once they were around the corner, a second set of doors came into view. The crying was coming through the open doorway. They rushed desperately through it and into a vast open space.

Dark-red carpet covered the floor. Circular pillars lined either side, carved with hideous monster decorations. Ore lamps hung from the walls, casting pale-white light. Straight ahead was a higher platform, in the center of which sat a very ornate chair. That had to be the throne that Emperor Vecta had returned to sit upon.

In the center of the room stood Iskahn and Sheyta, and beyond them was a monstrous black form—a minion with its wings spread.

And finally, a shadowy figure stood next to the throne. It wore a black hooded robe, but the sleeves and collar of the robe were vague and smoky, hiding the wearer's details. The figure was skinny but very tall. There was a dagger in its right hand, glowing a venomous purple shade, the tip of which was pointed at the baby cradled in its left arm.

Leazetta's cries were weak, and her face was scrunched up. She'd been exposed to this freezing cold for over two hours, so her life had to be significantly diminished. They needed to save her at once, but they couldn't afford to be careless now. The rage and haste were palpable in Sheyta's and Iskahn's stances.

The robed kidnapper spoke in an alien voice that sounded like some kind of beast or bird attempting to form human words, its mouth unfit for speech.

"…Ah, so it was the swordsman delegate who cut the chain. You are more trouble than even the stories say…"

It was impossible to gauge the age or race of the speaker. But there was one thing that was very clear.

"So…you're a man! Then you're *not* a dark mage!!" shouted Iskahn. The kidnapper laughed, making an eerie hissing noise.

"From what I hear, men use sacred arts in the human realm, yes? So a man can be a dark mage, can he not?"

"Wait…I recognize that poisoned blade…You're with the assassins guild!"

"Are you certain…? Anyone can use this sword. I might even be a pugilist you drove out of the guild." The kidnapper laughed mockingly again, then immediately turned chilly. *"The time for talk is over. I'll have to forget about the public execution, but I still mean to collect the delegate's head. Ambassador, use that slicing hand of yours to cut it off, or your daughter dies."*

A gray hand extended from the black sleeve, bringing the dagger closer to Leazetta's face. Iskahn and Sheyta went completely stiff.

At that very moment, something twanged, and the tip of the poisoned blade deflected sideways. A white ball of light surrounded

Leazetta's entire body. The kidnapper nearly dropped the baby altogether but quickly readjusted their hold on her.

Leazetta hadn't done anything, of course. Next to Ronie, Kirito's right hand was outstretched toward the throne and glowing the same color. He was protecting the baby with a barrier made of Incarnation.

"Sheyta! Iskahn!" he shouted, his voice pained. "I won't last long! Hurry..."

"I'm on it!!" shouted Iskahn, his body throwing off a light like burning flames.

The man in the black robe gave a strange, unintelligible command. The minion reacted to it.

"*Bshooo!*" the monster roared, but the sound was drowned out by the pugilist's bellow. "*Raaaaaaaah!!*"

Iskahn charged forward with tremendous force, driving his flaming fist into the minion's stomach. The monster's large body bent as the impact traveled in waves outward from its belly to its limbs.

It exploded, shedding a tremendous amount of filthy black blood, like a leather skin bursting when overfilled with liquid. Iskahn crossed his arms in front of his body to protect against the spraying poison.

A slender shadow then shot around Iskahn's back. Having been protected from the direct path of the blood by her husband, Sheyta charged at the throne, a gray blur.

"...!!"

With a silent scream, her left hand shot forth. The right arm of the kidnapper, holding the purple dagger, came loose from the shoulder and fell to the floor. Sheyta readied her right hand to chop off the remaining arm, which was holding her baby.

But within the darkness of the hood, something small flashed near the mouth.

A blowgun.

She quickly lifted her hand to block the dart, but her slender body immediately toppled.

The man in the black robe readjusted Leazetta in her protective ball of light and rushed to the left of the throne, gliding over the carpet. There was nothing but black wall in that direction, however. There was no escape for him.

Except…

A number of thoughts burst through Ronie's mind, and the moment they added up to one picture, she was on the run with her sword out.

In the distance, the kidnapper was charging right for the wall, his black robe whipping behind him. A large jewel below his neck glowed a brilliant scarlet color.

A part of the wall flashed the same color. A square portion of the obsidian wall began to rise with a sound like heavy rocks scraping one another…like a stone pestle being ground against a mortar.

The kidnapper rushed for the window that should not have been there, carrying Leazetta.

The distance to the attacker was over ten mels. It wasn't a distance Ronie could cover in a single leap with her leg strength.

But she would reach it. She would make sure of it.

"Yaaaaaaa!!" Summoning all her strength and willpower, she leaped forward with a wild scream.

She readied her new sword. When it went completely still, fusing with her arm as one shape pointed at a very specific height and angle, the blade began to glow light blue.

Ronie's body accelerated as though pushed by invisible hands. She left a bright trail in the air as she crossed ten mels in a single blink.

This was the Aincrad style's ultra-charging thrust, Sonic Leap.

Kirito had taught her both the move and what its sacred-tongue name meant—and the lesson paid off as she severed the left arm of the kidnapper from the shoulder.

At that moment, Kirito's barrier of Incarnation disappeared, hurtling Leazetta into the air unprotected. The man in the black robe did not stop running, despite the loss of his arms and so much blood. He leaped toward the window.

If she had performed another technique, she might have been able to defeat the kidnapper once and for all. But Ronie chose instead to stop and catch the baby.

The interloper shot through the window headfirst and vanished, melting into the morning light. Meanwhile, Ronie caught Leazetta firmly with her left arm and clutched the baby to her chest. She immediately crouched, laying her sword on the ground, and covered the pitifully wailing child with both arms to provide her with warmth.

"...I know, poor Lea, that was very scary. But it's okay...You're safe now...," she murmured, rubbing cheek against cheek. Eventually, the crying calmed down, and a tiny hand touched Ronie's face. On her left she heard the sound of the window closing again.

Ronie continued to hold the baby until someone came and put a hand on her back.

10

Despite a hundred guards searching for half a day, the body of the kidnapper was never found.

He had jumped out of the castle from a height of five hundred mels with his arms cut off. It would have seemed an impossible task to survive such a situation, but neither Iskahn, Sheyta, nor Kirito intended to assume the best-case scenario when it came to this incident.

At four o'clock in the afternoon, after the cleanup of the incident inside the castle had concluded, the four of them gathered in Sheyta and Iskahn's room again, where the window had since been repaired.

Leazetta was peacefully drinking milk in Sheyta's arms, the horrible ordeal completely forgotten. The palace's doctor and Sheyta, with her skill in high-level arts, were very thorough in determining that the baby wasn't under the effects of any poison or dark arts, thankfully.

On the other hand, they knew next to nothing about the kidnapper himself. And the biggest mystery of all—how he had opened the window on the fiftieth floor, which was controlled only by Emperor Vecta—remained unsolved.

"You know...it might be totally unrelated," said Ronie as she sipped an unfamiliar type of tea that smelled faintly of apples, "but I noticed that when he opened the window, the large jewel hanging around his neck glowed red."

"Red jewel…?" Kirito repeated. Sheyta looked curious as well. They did not seem to recognize the concept.

But Iskahn, who was just biting into a large slice of nut pie, frowned and muttered, "A glowing red jewel…Do you remember the particular shade of red, Ronie?"

She realized this was the first time the high-ranking man had confidently called her by name. "It was, um, not very bright…A darker red, the color of the setting sun or blood," she told him.

"Bloodred…No…it couldn't be……"

"Whoa, Iskahn, you can't just drop a hint like that and leave us hanging! It's against the rules!" Kirito complained.

"Against *what* rules…?" Iskahn growled, looking suspicious. But still he explained, "There was a stone like that embedded in Emperor Vecta's crown when he arrived before the war. I remember it because it was the only jewel he wore."

"Vecta's crown…? Then it *definitely* can't be. The first time he died was in battle with Commander Bercouli, thousands of kilors to the south of us. When he came back after that, he wasn't wearing the crown anymore. So whatever he was wearing the first time would have vanished on that rocky mountain down south."

"But you didn't see it happen, did you?" Iskahn retorted.

"Well…true…," Kirito murmured.

At the time, Kirito had been in a mentally inactive state. Bercouli and Vecta's duel to the death had been witnessed only by Alice the Integrity Knight, and she was no longer present in the Underworld.

Alice had transported Bercouli's body by dragon, and Kirito had taken it from her at the World's End Altar and delivered it back to the human realm. His remains now slept beneath a gravestone in the center of the garden in the southeast corner of the cathedral grounds.

"…True, I didn't perform a search of the place where Bercouli and Vecta fought. It would be hard to even identify the spot now…," Kirito admitted. He turned and looked out the window. "But…if it was the jewel's power that opened and closed the fiftieth-floor window, then you might be right: It could be Vecta's jewel. That doesn't explain who got it back and how…or who that man was…You mentioned the assassins guild in the throne room. What's that organization like?"

Iskahn gulped down his tea in one go and proclaimed with disgust, "Just what it sounds like: They perform assassinations for a living. They use poisons…The leader when the ten lords were around was a guy named Fu Za, and he died when General Shasta tried to stage a rebellion. That was a huge blow to the guild, and they're not even part of the Council of Five now. I'd almost completely forgotten about them…But if the guy in the robe is from the assassins guild, and he's got a minion doing his bidding, we've got a real fishy situation on our hands…"

"We should do a full investigation on them and the missing dark mages," Sheyta instructed.

"Yes," he agreed. "I intend to talk with the knighthood and the commerce guild, too. I don't want any more nonsense happening in Obsidia."

Kirito leaned forward and suggested, "About that—shouldn't we ask for the dark mages guild's help? After hearing about what Dee Eye Ell did, I don't necessarily blame you for giving the dark mages the cold shoulder…but I think you should try to repair that relationship and get them to guard the palace, too. With just armed guards, you're too susceptible to dark arts."

"As usual, you have a way of saying just what I don't want to hear," Iskahn said with a grimace. He shrugged and admitted, "But I guess you have a point. If all the humans in Obsidia are at one another's throats, we can't expect to solve any problems with demi-humans…How long are you going to stay here, Kirito?"

This time, it was Iskahn who was leaning forward and Kirito who was backing away. "I-I'd love to offer you all the help I can… but I'm going back to the human side tonight. We still haven't solved the problem over there, either…"

"Ah yes; that's true. On the other hand, I haven't been able to properly thank you for getting Leazetta back for us, and there's so much good food to be had…"

The sight of Iskahn pursing his lips like a child being deprived of playtime put a fond smile on Kirito's face that also contained the faintest note of grief.

"Wh-what's that expression for?"

"Oh…you just sounded like an old, old friend of mine, Iskahn. But look, the meeting's still next month, right? We'll come with a much bigger party next time."

"You bet! And get your stomach ready; I'll put together a menu of delicacies that'll make last night's dinner look like nothing… At any rate, you were a huge boon to have here. I'll never forget this debt I owe you for the rest of my life."

Iskahn stood up and stuck out his hand. Kirito straightened up and clasped it. From Sheyta's arms, Leazetta giggled and laughed at the sight of them.

After a few hours of sleep in their respective guest rooms, Kirito and Ronie ate a quick meal and left Obsidia Palace at eight o'clock in the evening.

This time, they didn't need to put anything on their faces or use Incarnation to fly. Sheyta flew them on Yoiyobi's back to where the dragoncraft was hidden.

Even reserved Sheyta looked stunned when she saw the steel dragon, but she grasped the capabilities of the dragoncraft right away. She said that she was looking forward to the day when such things would be mass-produced so that travel between the human realm and the Dark Territory would become easy. Then she returned to her home in the castle of obsidian, and Kirito and Ronie boarded the dragoncraft and flew into the western sky.

When the craft was flying and stable, Kirito exhaled slowly in the front seat and said, "That Sonic Leap you pulled off to get Leazetta back from the kidnapper was incredible, Ronie. When did you get so good at it?"

"Huh...I—I don't know. I was just desperate...," she stammered, tracing the silver hilt of her sword, which was resting between her seat and the wall. "I feel like...the sword gave me power. I would never be able to jump that distance under normal circumstances."

"I see...That means it's a good sword."

"I know." Ronie rested back against the seat.

The windshield of the dragoncraft offered a view of the Dark Territory's night sky as it flew quietly along. The stars were fewer in comparison to the human realm, but the moon was large and pale, a crescent slice in the sky directly overhead.

Despite the huge distance between the places we live, the people on both sides are looking up at the same moon...

At that very moment, she once again had the same eerie feeling that she'd gotten when she saw the sign on the inn in Obsidia and heard the melody of the bell tower. And this time, Ronie knew what it was.

"Um...Kirito?"

"What is it?"

"Why do the human realm and the dark realm both use the same words and letters? There was almost no communication between the two worlds from the very birth of the Underworld, so you would think they'd have completely different languages..."

It was something she'd never second-guessed before, but now that she had seen some of the great wide world for herself, she wanted to know the reason why it worked that way.

The swordsman from the real world was silent for a while. Eventually, he said, "Let's see...The real-worlders who created this place wanted the two realms to fight each other, so it should have been more convenient for their purposes to have the two worlds use completely different languages. After all, if you can't understand each other, you can never *find* understanding and make peace. But they—or something aside from the real-worlders—intentionally shared the same language between them. I don't know the reason why. But it's possible that it was for the purpose of bringing about a world that managed to move beyond hostility and fighting......"

Ronie found it hard to understand what he was saying. But she chose to keep thinking about it, rather than ask him to elaborate further.

The moon in the sky was another huge sphere, just like their world, Kirito had said. That was why it glowed with the light from Solus and waxed and waned.

If people lived on the moon, they would see the earth, where Ronie lived, as another glowing crescent. Would the people of the moon speak the same language, too? Like the people here, would they make many regrettable mistakes and shed blood but still do their best and wish for a better world?

The crescent moon above felt like a cradle capable of nurturing much life now. She reached up toward it.

But soon, she dropped her hand back to the hilt of her sword. "Um, Kirito?"

"Hmm...?"

"I've decided on a name for my weapon. I'll call it the Moon... the Moonbeam Sword."

"I see. That's a good name. I'm sure it will protect you well," he said. She flashed a bright smile and agreed, then wiped away tears that had come to her eyes unbidden.

I want to see Tiese, she realized. *I want to go to my friend trapped between love for the late Eugeo and the proposal from Renly and tell her the things I learned and considered on this journey.*

Somehow, Kirito seemed to sense this desire of hers, because he picked up the speed of the dragoncraft just a bit.

Like that, the steel dragon flew on and on to the west, gleaming in the pale moonlight.

(The End)

AFTERWORD

Thank you for reading *Sword Art Online 19: Moon Cradle*.

This story is treated as a kind of follow-up to the Alicization saga that ended in Volume 18, but that term might be a bit misleading, so I'd like to explain the concept further. (Beware of spoilers for this book beyond this point!)

In the middle of Volume 18, the Underworld entered the maximum-acceleration phase, meaning that, inside it, time passed at five million times the speed of the real world. Kirito and Asuna were left behind during that time, and they spent two hundred years in the Underworld before logging out. The *Moon Cradle* story takes place very early within that two-hundred-year span. In other words, less than five days pass over the course of Volume 19, but in the real world, it's one five-millionth of that time: just 0.08 seconds.

But even though it takes place in the blink of an eye, I'm sorry to say there will be one more book of it! In the following volume, the story will return to Centoria, where Kirito and Ronie and Asuna should be facing off against the mastermind of this plot. I want to get it out as soon as possible, so just bear with me until then.

I'd like to add a little more background to this story.

In the book, Ronie is imagining the numbers she and Tiese will get as Integrity Knights. Some readers might have wondered, "Wouldn't Eugeo be Thirty-Two?" As a matter of fact, although his memories were blocked by Administrator, and he called himself Eugeo Synthesis Thirty-Two, he regained those memories in the fight with Kirito and then died in battle against Administrator immediately following that. At the point when *Moon Cradle* takes place, Kirito is the only person who knows about all of this, and he has not told anyone that Eugeo was an Integrity Knight. So the number Thirty-Two wasn't retired, and Tiese will eventually inherit it.

I doubt that I'll get to it in the following volume, but I would like to write about Ronie's and Tiese's official promotions into the knighthood and the outcome of their love lives—eventually.

About a week after the release of this book, on February 18th, 2017, the animated feature film *Sword Art Online the Movie: Ordinal Scale* will hit theaters. Unlike all the other stories, which take place in VRMMOs, this one is set in an AR (augmented reality) game, but it's completely packed with unbelievable visuals, so I urge you to check it out on the big screen! Also, I'm sorry to abec and Miki for cutting it so close to the deadline once again! Hope to see you in the next volume!!

Reki Kawahara—January 2017